"A good book is the best of friends, the same today and forever."

—Tupper

Given for the glory of God
to the media library
in honor of

MR. STERLING REYNOLDS

with love and deep appreciation by

MR. & MRS. ERNEST REYNOLDS

HIS SON AND WIFE

SUMMER 1987 date

Young Man
Young Man

Young Man
Young Man
Eda Stertz

ZONDERVAN PUBLISHING HOUSE
A Division of The Zondervan Corporation
Grand Rapids, Michigan

For

IRA C. KLARER

who no doubt graces a special place in heaven
as much as she once graced a special place on earth.

Young man —
Young man —
Your arm's too short to box with God.

    *   *   *

And the young man journeyed on his way,
And he said to himself as he travelled along:
This sure is an easy road,
Nothing like the rough furrows behind
my father's plow.

Excerpt from
James Weldon Johnson's
"The Prodigal Son"
God's Trombones
The Viking Press 1927
New York City
(permission for use
  pending)

Young Man
Young Man

1

OCLONEE SWELTERED in the heat of the early afternoon as the Rev. Nathan E. Waite drove through its outskirts toward town. The shady yards of the small houses and their sagging porches were empty. Under the porches dogs slept in the striped shade, their noses buried in the sand.

Most of the cars moving along the street with him had licenses from other states. *They're vacationers on their way to the beaches,* Nathan thought. *They're passing through, but I'm not; this metropolis is my very own parish.* He could imagine the cracks Turner Harrison, his seminary roommate, would make and was glad he was not here to make them.

Turner had already assumed duties in his own first fulltime church. It was a small congregation, but in a growing, prestige neighborhood in Atlanta, the kind of thing Nathan had coveted.

He shrugged. All he needed was time. Little old Oclonee First was going to do all kinds of significant things under his expert guidance and boost him right into something big.

He had no trouble finding the house where he would board; it was right next to the church. He parked in the shade of a row of sycamores and in an almost reflex action checked himself out in the rear view mirror.

His appearance was more than adequate. He was as good looking as he needed to be. He had thick dark hair and black eyes the girls called expressive. His clothes were good in quality and style. Just looking at him, no one would guess he was the son of an ignorant country preacher.

As he climbed out of the car his future landlady came out on the porch, smiling widely, drying her hands in her apron. Cora Haynie was short and she was round — round face, round eyes behind smogged-over glasses, and a plump, round body. She came to clasp his hand warmly in her damp one and then, talking steadily, she led him up the stairs of her narrow entry hall to his room.

She had given him a large front bedroom on the side of the house next to the church. The room was furnished with old style furniture — plain, uncomfortable, and depressingly familiar. Nathan knew from having slept on one like it at home that the bed would be too short.

Cora watched him anxiously, smoothing her short hands down the apron tied around her plump middle. "Everything all right?"

"Everything's fine, Mrs. Haynie."

"I tried to fix it up for you some." She nodded at a large, vivid print hanging over the boarded-up fireplace. "Do you like the picture?"

"Oh, I do."

"It's a genuine copy of Christ in the Garden."

"What about that? You've been very thoughtful, Mrs. Haynie."

"Well, I'm proud to have you stay here, Brother Waite. We did have a parsonage, y'know, but it burned down last winter after Brother LeRoy left. Wasn't much of a loss actually. We'll get a new one built by and by — when you get married?"

"Oh, there's no hurry about a new parsonage. I'm sure I'll be very comfortable here." The room was pretty grim, but it was cool and clean. It would do for now.

"I haven't got but one other boarder just now, that's El'na Boyette, a school teacher. She just moved in with me, y'know."

"Really?" Now that was an interesting coincidence.

"Yes, El'na had a bad thing happen to her about three years ago. Shocked the whole town. She and Buddy Warren was engaged to be married, had been nearly all their lives, and then Buddy up and eloped with El'na's little sister Sarah Sue. It was terrible for El'na. The girls were orphans, y'know."

Of course they were orphans. What a soap opera that must have been.

"Buddy and Sarah Sue's been living in Anderson since, had their first baby there, and El'na's stayed right by herself in the old homeplace until just the other evening when she came over here crying — saying she couldn't stand staying alone another night." She turned abruptly to an earlier theme. "A preacher needs a helpmate, I always say. I expect a man your age has somebody in mind."

Nathan hesitated just a moment. Then he went over to his suitcase and got out a picture of Julia Harrison. It was the same picture Turner had kept on his desk their three years together at the seminary. Nathan had always wondered if Turner's sister could possibly live up to the promise of the picture. After this summer's visit to the Harrison's home in Atlanta Nathan knew. She could, and his own love life had developed a distinct new sense of direction. Of course Julia didn't know that yet.

He had asked Turner for the picture very casually, more aware than ever of the Harrison money and social position.

"I've grown accustomed to her face," he quipped.

"Take it," Turner said. "They're all over the house." He paused. "They're also on assorted desks in Atlanta and adjoining cities. You know that though, don't you?"

Nathan felt put down but he grinned. "Of course. I have to get in line. Any objections?"

"None whatsoever. In fact, I think my little sister is fascinated with you. You're a slightly different breed of cat than the guys she's been dating."

"It's my farmer's charm," Nathan said. Turning, he let his grin fade. He means I'm no breed at all, probably. He slipped the picture into his suitcase wishing he hadn't asked for it, and then snapped the suitcase shut. The devil with Turner.

Cora had moved to his side and was looking eagerly at the picture. "Your intended?" she asked.

Nathan hesitated again, briefly. "Intended? Yes, I guess that's a good word for this young lady."

With a light touch he steered Cora toward his door, explaining that he wanted to clean up before he went over to the church. Closing the door behind her he was delighted with his own cleverness. She couldn't say he had told her he was engaged — but she probably would. He grinned. He might need a little of that kind of insurance in this set-up.

Nathan didn't meet Eleanor until supper that night and at the end of the meal he didn't know her any better than he had at its beginning. She sat throughout the meal with scarcely a word, her wide-set gray eyes directed at her own plate, her mouth grave.

Nathan judged her to be about his age though her solemnity made her seem older, and very sedate. Her hair style, contrariwise, was very young. She had combed it straight back and fastened it with a wide silver barrette from which it hung in a straight and shining fall. Not bad looking actually, he thought, shaped up pretty good — but she was sending no signals in his direction. And that suited him just fine.

The door bell rang and Cora answered it. Nathan heard voices and Eleanor whispered, "Rena Petrie." Nathan got up at once, brushing his mouth hastily with his napkin.

In a moment Cora was back and Rena Petrie stood filling the dining room door. Nathan thought she must be the tallest woman he'd ever known. When she walked in the room her bosom came first like the prow of a ship, with the rest of her following majestically behind.

"Good evening, Reverend Waite," she said, fixing her black eyes on his. "You don't remember me I'm sure."

Nathan extended his hand and bowed a little. "Of course, I remember you, Mrs. Petrie. Your husband is chairman of the Board of Deacons, and you teach a ladies Bible class."

Rena acknowledged this with something similar to a smile. "I teach the Philatheas," she said, "the largest class."

Nathan watched Rena's inspection of the room. She seemed to disapprove of the food on the table and of Eleanor to whom she had not yet spoken. She stared a moment at the girl, raised her eyebrows slightly and sniffed, "Good evening, Eleanor."

"Good evening, Mrs. Petrie, how are you?"

"Well enough." She turned back to Nathan. "Mr. Petrie is out of town and asked me to welcome you in his place. We both trust you will have a successful ministry here." She frowned a little at Cora and Eleanor as if they represented some sort of obstacle to that success. "Well, I must go," she added with another sniff.

Nathan followed her down the hall to see her out. At the door she took his hand and drew him close to her jutting bosom. Her face as stern as death itself she asked, "Has Cora told you about the dreadful thing that happened here last week?"

Nathan shook his head questioningly. He wasn't sure whether she had told him or not. Several things she had told him sounded on the dreadful side.

Rena's face filled with scorn. "I'll let her tell you her story first, I'm sure she has one, and I'll talk with you about it later myself." She patted the hand which Nathan had been thinking of retrieving. "Good night now, I hope you rest as well as possible."

When she had released him and gone Nathan walked back to the dining room. Eleanor had left and Cora was clearing the table, her mouth pursed and angry. He started to say a quick good night, not really wanting to get in on whatever was an obvious conflict between the women. Cora did not let him off.

"I couldn't help overhearing what Rena said. She couldn't leave a thing like that rest to save her soul." She crashed a stack of dishes together. "You might as well know to start with, Preacher, Rena's got a nose for sin like a hound dog for rabbits. Most of the time she sniffs at nothing, but she's on a hot trail this time."

She paused and took a deep breath. "I wasn't going to tell you right off, you being new and all, but last week I ran smack dab into a couple making love right in the church!"

"Well, that's not the most unusual thing in the world," Nathan said, relieved the trouble was not over an embezzling treasurer or something serious like that.

"Preacher! This wasn't just kids smooching. This was two grown-up people that should'na been near each other."

"Oh. Well, that does make a difference."

"I reckon it does. It got out right away because Billy Thompson, that's the man, was so rattled when he realized I'd seen them that he went straight home and confessed to his wife Effie that he was mixed up with another woman — but he wouldn't tell her which woman. Effie left him on the spot. The next day Billy came to me and tried to get me to promise I wouldn't tell on the girl either. Rena happened to see him here and with that uncanny way she has of putting two and two together decided I was in on the secret, and told Effie and her folks. Now the Lesters are nearly as mad at me as they are at Billy, and my church friends, especially Myrtle, have been calling me all week worrying me to tell."

She paused for breath or advice, he wasn't sure which. She probably wanted to go on and tell him the girl's identity, to get the burden off her own shoulders. He didn't want it. The affair had happened before he came and he wanted to stay out of it.

He moved to go, hoping to end the discussion. "Well, this is probably one of those mole hills made into a mountain, Mrs. Haynie. It'll probably clear up in a few days." He gave her a smile which she returned without enthusiasm. "Good night, then," he added, "and thanks for everything."

It was a great relief to finally get in bed even if he did have to lie catty-cornered to stretch full length. He was tired. And for perfectly legitimate reasons, like driving most of the day to get here, and spending the rest of it meeting new people and new situations.

Certainly he wasn't tired because of his futile efforts to sort those people and situations and hang them as neatly on their proper pegs as he had hung his clothes. Certainly he was not anxious.

He glanced up behind him at the high carved headboard of the old fashioned bed.

Looked like a blasted tombstone at night.

A beam from the street light in front of the house cut through his window and ran in a bright panel across the end of the bed and up the middle of the boarded up fireplace, eerily lighting Cora's "original copy of Christ in the Garden." That picture had to go, as soon as he could find a way to get rid of it without hurting the widow's feelings.

The edge of the panel cut through Julia's picture lighting one eye and a swirl of blond hair. Nathan squinted, trying to bring the total picture within his vision.

Then he sighed.

Atlanta was a million light years away.

14

2

NATHAN WENT to see Aunt Sally Lennon, the oldest member of his congregation, on Saturday, partly because she had already called Cora's house three times to inquire as to his whereabouts, but largely because Rena Petrie had asked him to.

Settling into his office at the church he had decided the only thing for him to do was take a positive, aggressive approach to the church and its members. If he ignored the scandal that had disturbed the church's slumber and at the same time tossed the people some new challenges to talk about he could knock off a couple of problems with the same action.

As for Rena, he had been wary of her from their first encounter back in the summer when he had come to Oclonee to preach his trial sermon. But he was a realist. Rena came with the church. If wooing her a little would give him peace to accomplish what he wanted to accomplish he would woo. He would start by making this call early as she had requested.

He found Aunt Sally living in an old frame house full of cats, crocheted doilies and religious literature. She met him at the door, leaning on a man's gold handled cane, and led him through the house to a side porch where they sat on plastic covered cushions in wicker chairs. On the edge of the porch a sentinel row of spindly geraniums guarded the rail.

"In the old days I would have had you for dinner," Aunt Sally shouted in a clarion voice. "I always used to have my preacher and his family in for dinner. I used to do a lot of things. I was a power at the church — I don't mind saying it. Can't do anything anymore. The most I can hope for is to get to church now and then when somebody thinks to come after me."

She thumped her cane at a large yellow cat that was rubbing a fat side against his pants legs. The cat promptly jumped in his lap, trampled his legs until she had kneaded out a hollow and then curled up and went to sleep.

Aunt Sally leaned over and tapped the leg that was free of cat, as if his attention might have wandered. "I've got five diseases," she announced. "None of them's contagious, thank God."

At first Nathan tried to do a little of the talking. He soon realized that not only did the old lady not hear him well, she herself was too deprived of the opportunity to talk to discipline herself to the politeness of listening to someone else. Or perhaps she had never listened to anyone else. From then on he rocked, patted the cat and listened. This was his first call in Oclonee. He intended to give satisfaction.

"We really miss Brother LeRoy. That's a good man if ever there lived one. Used to come by here every week. Even brought my medicine from the drug store if I didn't have any other way to get it. Brother LeRoy knew I was a worker long as I was able. He was a good preacher, too, knew his Bible."

She tapped his knee again. "They didn't fill you full of that liberalism stuff at the seminary, did they? My old daddy used to say a preacher didn't need to go to the seminary. All he needed was a Scofield Bible and a dictionary."

She gazed at him a moment working her long jaw as if settling her teeth more comfortably. "I was the first teacher of the Philathea class. When my health gave out I turned it over to Rena Petrie. Just like Elijah in the Bible I gave her my mantle. She's a smart girl. Bossy, but smart. I knew she'd keep that class in line."

She leaned forward. "Young man, take a piece of advice from one of your oldest church members. When you want to know which way the wind's blowing you check the vane at Rena's house." She nudged his foot with her cane. "You know what I mean?"

"Well, yes, Aunt Sally . . ."

"You heard about the scandal?"

Startled at her candor he nodded that he had and then added that he thought it was a shame.

"It's been years since we had such a thing happen in our church, years. Sure gives folks a lot to talk about. The shenanigans by themselves would have been enough to keep 'em occupied for weeks, but then we got this mystery. Cora told you who the girl is?"

He shook his head.

"She'll tell sooner or later. Corrie Haynie never kept a secret in her life. 'Course I got my own ideas. Corrie's keeping her mouth shut can only mean one thing. She's trying to protect somebody. Why? She didn't waste any time protecting El'na when Buddy ran off. She had that tale over town before they cleared the city limits. Did you know she saw that elopement actually happen? Well, she did. Standing on her porch she saw Buddy and Sarah Sue get in his car and drive off. Don't that beat all?" She meditated a moment, working her teeth. "Rena will get to the bottom of it."

He patted the cat.

In a moment a car pulled up to the curb in front of Aunt Sally's house and a thin woman in a swirling, flowered dress got out. She looked vaguely familiar.

Aunt Sally glanced over the geraniums. "It's Alberta Peeples," she announced, "our choir director." She leaned forward and spoke in a stage conspirator's whisper. "Alberta stays just one step ahead of a fit."

Nathan eased the cat to the floor and stood up as Alberta rushed onto the porch.

"Hellooo, Aunt Sally," she cried and then put her hand over her breast as if startled at seeing him, when Nathan knew he must certainly have been in plain view from the sidewalk. "Why, Brother Waite! What a lovely surprise. I hadn't dreamed of seeing you before tomorrow." She trilled a laugh like a C-scale on a binge.

"It's good to see you again, Miss Peeples. I remember.you from this summer."

"Oh . . . you do make a girl feel good." She went over to stand by Aunt Sally. "Isn't it just wonderful to have a preacher again, Aunt Sally? And such a handsome one." She waved a scolding finger at Nathan. "I tell you we girls are a mite jealous of Eleanor." She nervously ran her scale of laughter again. "I shouldn't have said that . . . in the light of everything." 17

She wagged her fingers at him again. "You just don't pay

any attention to me. I'm a great tease. Tell him I'm a great tease, Aunt Sally."

"What's that?"

"Nothing, dear." She leaned over to speak directly into Aunt Sally's ear. "I ran into Durwood and he said to tell you he would pick you up Sunday for church. He thought you'd want to go on Brother Waite's first Sunday."

Aunt Sally nodded and Alberta smiled archly at Nathan. "Durwood Thigpen is one of our eligible young men." She patted Aunt Sally's shoulder. "Well, I must go — a thousand things to do before tomorrow."

Nathan remained standing after she'd rushed out. He'd had about enough of this particular call.

Aunt Sally pushed herself up. "Alberta's bound to run into Durwood every now and then. She chases him night and day."

At the door she leaned both hands on her cane and looked up at him. "Well, I'm glad Durwood's taking me to church. I want to hear you preach, but you'll have to go some to out-preach Brother LeRoy. That's a good man if one ever lived."

Nathan didn't see Mr. Petrie until seconds before the organ began playing for the worship hour on Sunday morning. He had been up since dawn savoring the excitement and confusion of his first Sunday at First Baptist. Mr. Petrie, an extremely tall man with fine silvery hair, was obviously neither excited or confused. He led the opening exercises of the worship hour with a detached air and welcomed Nathan to the pulpit with an absolute minimum of words. It was a somewhat deflating experience.

During the special music preceding his sermon Nathan made the mistake of reappraising the condition of the sanctuary. This really was depressing. Fumes from the heating system had painted shadows on the ivory walls and dampness from a leaky roof had ringed the ceiling and caused the paint to flake off in places. Nathan thought the church should have painted the sanctuary in self-pride before he came, but since they hadn't the project would take top priority on his own list. He had no intention of inviting outside speakers or even his friends to come until the place was cleaned up.

The special music crashed to a halt and Mr. Petrie left the podium. And now the platform was Nathan's. The people sitting before him looked to him expectantly, a hush fallen upon them. Standing in this pulpit as pastor for the first time, Nathan suddenly felt more hushed than the people. His people. Most of them he did not know. Their failings and anxieties were securely hidden behind their Sunday faces. If a modern Jezebel sat before him she looked just like her more innocent sisters. And what she had done was past history as far as he was concerned.

It soon became obvious to him the past was not history to the congregation. They listened to his beautifully worked out sermon, apparently just long enough to determine that he was not going to preach on a subject related to last week's shocker, and then simply tuned him out.

Rena listened in her pew, but not to him. To whom, Nathan wondered, a voice from heaven? Cora looked distinctly bothered and occasionally Eleanor cast a sympathetic glance in her direction.

Most of the women sat worrying their earrings or picking at their gloves, their eyes roving the parts of the church within their lines of vision. Men sat with arms folded watching him with impassive faces or leaned on their hymn books staring at the backs of the heads in front of them. A row of teenagers on the back seat giggled and passed notes throughout the sermon.

Nathan thought grimly, *I've been upstaged by Cora's rabbits.*

Standing at the door afterward he received few comments to treasure from the people passing by. The general remark from the women was that he had preached a sweet message. A few of the men seemed genuinely glad to welcome him, but a number of them were uncommittal both as to his arrival and his welcome, shaking his hand without quite meeting his eye. *They all act like they're guilty of something,* Nathan thought, *and I bet Bill Thompson isn't even here.*

Out on the sidewalk Nathan could see people standing in little groups whispering and looking over their shoulders keeping track of who might have roamed within earshot of the whispers. *I ought to preach tonight on "Thou Shalt Not*

Gossip," he thought. What a ridiculous situation.

He shook hands with the last person in line and pausing a moment heard Aunt Sally shout, "At times like these, a body wishes Brother LeRoy was still our preacher."

"Indeed a body does," Nathan murmured, walking briskly back into the sanctuary.

On his way to the Petries' for dinner Nathan stopped to speak to Cora who was serving up her own and Eleanor's meal with the same bothered look she'd worn in church.

"Rena told me she asked the Philatheas to pray for you," he said.

"Phttt," Cora hissed between her teeth.

"I appreciate your feelings. She shouldn't have embarrassed you in front of the class."

He adjusted his tie clip which hadn't needed it. "But now, Corrie, apart from her bad taste, let me ask you, have you given any serious thought to the fact that it might be better to have this whole affair out in the open? I know everybody abhors a tattle tale, but. . . ." He paused and looked up.

Cora was staring at him, chin out, mouth set.

He hastily buttoned his jacket. "Oh, well, like I said, everybody abhors a tattle tale."

Sunday dinner at the Petries' proved to be a tightly structured affair. The house itself was distinctly structured, built at a time when turrets and porches enclosed with ginger bread balusters spelled status.

"I, ah, admire your home," Nathan told Rena, taking an uncomfortable seat on a small couch covered with a spiky gold material. The couch gave not a whit to the weight of his body.

"This was my grandmother's house," Rena said. "This room is just as she left it."

That figures, Nathan thought. The polished, ornate interior looked as if a victorian wand had first furnished and then frozen it.

20

After getting him seated Rena turned into the adjoining dining room to catch hold of the arm of a young woman who had been hanging back by the table, ostensibly checking its place settings, and brought her to Nathan.

"This is my daughter Pauline — Mrs. Kenneth Beck. Kenneth works in the barber shop with his father Carlisle, who is one of our fine Sunday school teachers. His mother Gertrude is president of our women's work."

Nathan had risen and now leaned forward to shake hands with Pauline. She was nearly as tall as her mother, but very slender. She had her mother's coloring, but there was about her face a softness that Nathan doubted had ever graced Rena's. She would not quite look at him, pulled her hand quickly from his, and looked down at her feet. Looking at her Nathan thought of one word, vulnerable.

As they stood Samuel came in with Kenneth Beck. Slightly shorter than his wife, Kenneth had bright brown eyes that shifted quickly, like his body filled with restless energy unable to adjust to victorian furniture.

Throughout the dinner hour Rena dominated the conversation. She turned Nathan's attempted conversation with the young couple away from them as she told Nathan of her oldest daughter in Brunswick who had married well and was active in church and community. It was pitifully obvious that it was this daughter who most found favor in her mother's sight.

At first any mention Nathan made of the church brought to Rena's face a look of pain bordering on martyrdom. In the midst of one such pain she said, "Let us speak only of that which is pleasant concerning our dear church. I don't wish the young ears among us to hear conversation regarding that dreadful thing which has befallen us."

Nathan's mouth dropped. Wow! 35,000 Southern Baptist churches and he had to draw the one with this character in it! He looked at Kenneth who immediately turned his eyes toward the ceiling and pursed his lips with an air of beatification. Nathan closed his mouth with a snap, not sure whether Kenneth was making fun of Rena or himself.

As for "that dreadful thing," he had absolutely no thought of referring to it before ears of any age. He wanted to divert Rena from it completely — to the profound hibernation of the church, for example. Nathan was intent on plans for its awakening — change, improvement, that was what he wanted to talk about.

Samuel Petrie, the man to whom Nathan should most naturally appeal, filled him with something like awe. The man walked with such stateliness, his lean face at peace as if he moved in some better world above and beyond his fellows and his wife.

He sat the affair out, trying to express some of the same serenity as did his host, inwardly wiggling like Kenneth Beck wiggled, miserable on Rena's red velvet chair.

3

EARLY IN THE WEEK Nathan accepted an invitation to go fishing with a young businessman of the church. Not that Nathan was that eager to fish, he just wanted to get with a church member who acted like he wanted to go — anywhere.

Unexpectedly, he ran into disapproval from Cora. "It won't set too well with the church folks who might call if I tell 'em you're already on the river."

"Don't tell them I'm on the river. Just tell them I'm visiting with one of the young men of the church. They don't have to know where we're visiting."

She withheld her blessing. "Don't get too thick with Buck Stevens right off," she said. "He's not the most popular man at the church, y'know. Him and Alice are newcomers and some of the folks think he's pushy. And Alice ain't exactly backward. She, she . . ." Miraculously, Cora seemed at a loss for words and then suddenly found a stream of them. "She talks too much — speaks out at the business meetings. The men don't care for that, y'know."

Nathan knew.

Buck drove Nathan out to the Oclonee River where he had a shack and a boat. It was perfectly quiet there except for the incessant ring of the insects' chatter. Fallen trees trailed their branches in the slow moving current of the river, thick grass moved up from the bank and stretched its curling ends under the moss hung oaks near the shack. The shack belonged to its surroundings, gray as the gray of the oaks and moss, settling idly on its foundations as if it planned eventually to meld into the salt and pepper sand beneath it.

Buck maneuvered his boat quickly and easily to the spot down the river where he wanted it. Nathan watched, speculating on the picture of the Stevens Cora had drawn for him.

"I understand you and Alice are newcomers," he said.

Buck looked up and scowled, his scalp showing red through his cotton blond hair. "Newcomers! We've lived here nine years. Ninety wouldn't make us natives to the old guard. Any idea I try to project at the church is about as welcome as mosquitoes on a picnic."

"Typical small town provincialism."

"Maybe so, but it doesn't make it any easier to take. Old Brother LeRoy catered to the powers that be and there wasn't much I could get stirring. Now for the first time I've got some real hope. I think you're the man to rally the young crowd."

Nathan reflected grimly that at least a part of the young crowd had gotten a little too rallied in recent days. He pulled gently on his line. "You're not saying the church is divided into two camps?"

Buck laughed. "Oh, no. That's the trouble. There's only one camp here with a few permanent type officers. Those old coots have got it so sewed up there's no way either to change things or develop new leadership."

Nathan pulled impatiently on his line. "Well, of course we can't have that. I'll just have to get these 'old coots' as you call them to lead out in a more progressive program."

Buck laughed with what seemed to Nathan an unnecessary amount of doubt. "Preacher, you'd be wasting your time. Your hope is with the young crowd. Get to work on them."

After giving the situation careful thought the best part of two days Nathan decided Buck was at least partly right. As pastor he needed to develop leadership among the younger adults and the best way to do that was to organize them in small groups. He would, however, work through established channels when he could, and with that in mind he went by the Court House to see Henry Buchanan, his Sunday school superintendent.

24   Henry smiled broadly when he saw Nathan come in, and moved from behind his counter to shake hands with him. They sat down on a long black bench against the wall. The

room smelled of old papers, dried ink and tax papers of several accumulated generations.

Encouraged by Henry's smile Nathan plunged into the matter most directly on his mind. "I've been wondering if it wouldn't strengthen our Sunday school if we organized some new adult classes. To start with, we might break up the two biggest classes into smaller units."

Henry stopped smiling. "Mrs. Petrie wouldn't let you divide her class. Carlisle wouldn't like it either."

Nathan tried a new tack. "Well then, why not organize some completely new classes for people not now coming to Sunday school? For instance we might start a group for young women in their twenties . . ."

"That'd be the same as saying twenty-year-old women ain't coming because they don't like Rena Petrie."

"No, it wouldn't, it has nothing to do with Mrs. Petrie."

"You start fooling with the Sunday school you'll find out it has everything to do with Mrs. Petrie."

Nathan sighed. "Can we forget her just for a moment anyway? Don't you yourself think there would be some value in having several more classes for men and women — according to their ages, interests and so forth?"

Henry pursed his lips, looked back over his shoulder as if to be sure the office was still empty and then back at Nathan. "Might," he said.

"Well, can't you and I work together toward such a plan?"

Henry looked dolefully at Nathan. "Preacher, did you ever watch a mill hand run a log into a buzz saw?"

Nathan laughed. Henry didn't even smile, but sat tapping his fingers on his knees.

"Mr. Buchanan, does it occur to you at all that it's wrong for one person to have such control?"

Henry drummed with his fingers. "It occurs to me, preacher."

"But you won't do anything to change the set-up?"

"I'm not the kind of man for changing things. I'm just an ordinary clerk. I write out figures and send notices and sign receipts. All day long that's what I do." He stood up sighing. Walking around back of the counter he pulled a ledger toward the light. "Yes sir, I just send notices and sign receipts. I'm not much of a buzz saw man."

Nathan watched him helplessly. This interview had not been at all the sort of thing he had intended. He tried to hide how disgruntled he felt behind a hardy smile and a voice to match. "Well, you're busy, I'll move along. Good to talk to you, Henry, er, Mr. Buchanan."

A few days later Nathan was cleaning old literature out of his study when Rena appeared suddenly at his door.

She wasted no time with small talk. "Reverend Waite, I understand you've set out to divide the Philatheas."

"Why no, Mrs. Petrie," he stammered, "I hadn't actually planned..."

"I took that class under the leadership of the Holy Spirit. He has blessed and prospered my work with it. Any plan that would affect the Philatheas in any way smacks of the devil's influence. My women will stand as one, to fight the devil, in any form he might appear."

Nathan rubbed his fingers along his forehead half expecting to find the nubbins of horns. He was still rubbing when she left.

Well, he thought glumly, *at least I diverted her attention.*

After prayer meeting that night Nathan waylaid Buck on his way up to the choir loft to practice. Looking around to be sure no one was listening he said, "I just about got clobbered today."

"I know," Buck laughed, "I heard."

Nathan scowled. "Is nothing a secret in this town?"

"Nope."

"Well, anyway, I walked into it with Rena and I've got to walk out again."

"Do you?"

"I most certainly do. We'll just shift our attention, for the time being, to something else that needs doing."

They leaned against the back of a pew, their arms folded. Nathan tucked in his bottom lip as his eyes moved to the dirty ivory colored walls of the auditorium and then up to the ceiling where the paint was flaking away from the plaster.

"Uhhuh," Buck said, "you're right, but I have to warn you that it won't be easy. It's come up and been voted down a half dozen times since I've been here."

Nathan grinned at him. "Don't sell me short, old buddy. You said you thought I could rally the young crowd, well how about helping me rally them around this project? We can start after supper tomorrow night at the Marceau's house."

Nathan pulled up in the shallow sandy ditch by the edge of the Marceau's lawn with Buck's car right behind him. They all got out together. Alice Stevens was wearing a lime yellow sheath that was perfect with her burnished red hair. She carried a white sweater over her freckled arm. She returned Nathan's smile, and held his eyes a moment letting him know she appreciated his appreciation.

Buck stepped between them. Laying his hand on Nathan's arm he nodded to a tri-level next door to the Marceau's. "Just for your information, that's the Thompson's house. They would have been here tonight under other circumstances. They're part of our crowd."

"Let's go in," Alice said abruptly.

After dinner the men went to the patio while the girls did the dishes. Nathan did more listening than talking, assessing the young men's possible value in the church.

Buck was a natural leader, but he obviously did not have the confidence of the older people. The short and combustible Kenny Beck would be quick to speak out, maybe too quick, and Nathan wondered how defensive Kenny might turn if his elders were put under pressure. Al Marceau had been a Catholic when he married Dolly which had greatly upset her mother, according to Cora. His background probably accounted for his quietness tonight during several animated discussions about church affairs. Still, he had been baptized into the church and so represented one vote.

"You're mighty quiet tonight," Buck said a little impatiently.

"I was just thinking about something I want done at the church."

Buck sat forward grinning. "Let us in on it then."

"I think one of the things we need to do right away is

redecorate the sanctuary. What would you say to that, Al?"

Al looked down at his feet. "Sure needs it."

"It's been needing it," Kenny burst out. "Our kindly treasurer Ashley Poole has always killed it, says we can't afford it."

Buck was sitting erect, his cotton blond hair standing up from his head against the evening breeze. "Ashley can stuff it. We got a new preacher now and I'm going to use his newness as a ram rod to get this thing pushed through."

"Calm yourself, honey, calm yourself," Alice said, coming out onto the patio with the other women. "Right now nobody's pushing through anything. We're going to sit right here and rest easy."

They had taken her cue and were sitting loosely in the plastic strapped chairs, chatting as casually as the breeze that intermittently caressed and deserted them when a car drove up to the tri-level next door. Conversation ceased as a tall young woman got out and clicked on high heels up the sidewalk toward the house.

Dolly whispered to Nathan, "There's Effie."

Nothing else was said as they listened to her staccato steps to her front door. They heard the key in the lock and in a moment lights began to come on in the house.

Dolly was shaking her head, looking for all the world like Myrtle shaking her head at Cora over the whole sad affair.

Al cleared his throat. "Dolly, go ask her to come have a coke with us. You know she saw us sitting out here."

"Oh, I don't think so," Dolly said, and Pauline added quickly, "She wouldn't want to come."

"She can always say no," Al said.

Shaking her head again Dolly cut across the lawn to go into the tri-level and in a few minutes they saw the two women coming back.

Nathan had met Effie, but most of what he knew about her came via Cora. Effie was what the women called high-strung. She kept an immaculate house, dressed well, had her hair done in Anderson and wore very high heels on all occasions.

She came now and standing stiffly at the edge of the patio

acknowledged their greetings before speaking directly to Nathan.

"About a month ago Mr. Thompson..." she frowned slightly, "my father-in-law donated the paint to redo the furniture in my Sunday school room. He thought then that Bill...that some of the young men in the church might do the painting. I wonder if you would put a notice in the church news asking for volunteer help."

"Of course I will, Effie. As a matter of fact we were just talking about some painting that needs immediate attention. Maybe your smaller project will be contagious."

Effie didn't smile at his small joke, and left soon after.

Even when her car had driven away the group could not seem to relax. Nathan could understand that. These were Effie's closest friends. And Bill's.

Now that he had seen Effie again Nathan wondered if he'd ever actually seen Bill. He was almost certain he had not come to a service at church. It would have been impossible to miss the commotion his appearance would have caused.

What kind of a fellow was he? Nathan could not avoid casting him somewhat in the role of a sophisticated villain, though he hadn't noticed Oclonee First was overshadowed with sophistication. But then maybe that was why Bill had offered insurmountable temptation to one of the girls.

One of these girls?

Nathan refused to allow himself to speculate.

On the announced Tuesday evening for the volunteer painters to come and paint Effie's furniture Nathan put on old clothes and went over to the church right after supper. He planned to work on his prayer meeting talk until the other men came to paint.

He was annotating an outline when he heard someone come through the outside entrance into the basement, and in a moment heard the sounds of furniture moving and metallic scrapes as if someone were in the paint cans.

I've got an eager beaver on my hands, he thought, a little annoyed to be disturbed before the hour set for the paint crew to start work.

He kept doggedly at his outline until he heard a car pull

up outside the church and men's voices as they got out of it. He cleared his desk quickly and started for the basement.

A young man was hard at work in Effie's room. He sat on one small chair, his gangly legs at an awkward angle, and held another chair upside down, carefully applying the color. His sun bleached brown hair was awry and he whistled a tuneless, soft whistle as he worked.

Turning to dip his brush in the can of paint he saw Nathan standing in the door. He put the brush down across the can and uprighted the chair. Standing up he wiped his deeply tanned hands down the side of his jeans and came forward to shake Nathan's hand.

"I'm Billy Thompson," he said.

4

Running down the steps on his way to the fall business meeting Nathan found Cora and Eleanor in the hall getting their wraps from the hall tree. He put down his Bible and notes to hold Cora's sagging black sweater for her. "You girls listen close and vote right tonight," he said, hoping he didn't sound as tense as he felt.

He had thought once or twice of telling them Buck was going to bring up the matter of painting the sanctuary, but remembering Cora's antipathy toward Buck had decided against it.

Eleanor slipped into her soft suede jacket before he could help and swung her long hair to clear it from her collar. Her blouse, the same deep pink as her skirt, had a wide ruffle and tiny pearl buttons down the front. She was completely feminine, and completely aloof. He certainly didn't care. Well, he cared a little. He wasn't used to girls turning him off.

In the auditorium of the church a fair sized crowd bunched in the middle of the center section. Dr. Davison, because of his faulty hearing, sat on the second pew in front of where Nathan stood. Josephina, the Ponders' ten-year-old brat, had informed him that Dr. Davison really sat there to guard the collection plates.

Laura Adams came forward and took her place as church clerk. Nathan couldn't guess her age, but he thought she had probably been an old maid since early childhood. While she was reading the minutes in her sweet, precise voice Nathan watched Buck, sitting erect on the edge of his pew, one hand on the pew in front of him, scarcely able to wait for old business to be called for.

He was on his feet the first instant it became possible in the procedure. "Brother Waite, I've got some business that's been old a long time. We've talked and talked about painting this auditorium and a lot of us thought it ought to be done before our new preacher came. But we just couldn't seem to get going on it." He turned and smiled around at the people sitting in back of him. A few of the younger women returned his smile. "Now I happen to know from my own wife that women like to get things spruced up at this time of year before winter sets in, and I have a feeling that the ladies of this congregation would like to do some housecleaning in the Lord's house this fall. Brother Moderator, I move we paint this auditorium."

Nathan, a little concerned that Buck had moved too quickly, turned to recognize Ashley Poole who had risen to his feet before a second to Buck's motion could be made.

Ashley was tall and thin and his clothes hung loosely on him as if a thrifty mother still bought them big enough to allow for growth. His head, rising turtle-like from his loose collar, was ridged across the top emphasizing its bald state. His remaining hair he wore in a long fringe at the neck and ears. He had been a carpenter all of his adult life and the treasurer of the church for a sizeable portion of it.

Ashley stood fingering an emblem hanging from his watch chain with the long fingers of one hand, the other resting lightly on the pew in front of him.

"Well, now," he said. "It appears like there's always them that's over eager to spend the Lord's treasure. Especially some of the young crowd that don't know the meaning of money yet. We've been talking about this paint job for years now, and that's a fact. I told you when it first came up, we can't afford it. I tell you now we still can't unless somebody makes a large designated gift or some class takes it on as a project." He looked pointedly at Buck and sat down.

George Harrington raised his hand and Nathan recognized him, knowing he might as well. Harrington spoke at least once and always at some length on any matter coming up before any group of which he was a part, usually not adding or detracting a great deal, but managing in the interim to set everybody's teeth on edge with irritation.

"I agree with Brother Poole," he said in his light, uneven voice. "We can't afford to paint and besides, what we really need to do is mend the roof. It's been leaking longer than the church has needed painting. Maybe we ought to take a special collection, although I know people don't like to hear money, money, money every time they come to church. Still, the roof has to be mended and I have to admit the sanctuary does look bad, but on the other hand, we never have gotten new gutters."

He was speculating on how to raise the money for new gutters when his exasperated wife finally pulled hard enough on his coat tails to get him to sit down.

Nathan immediately recognized Alma Warren when she fluttered her tiny hand with the three diamond rings at him. She was one of the few members of the church who could herself have the sanctuary painted if she so desired.

Fingering the collar of her dress she suggested the whole matter be tabled until next year when it would be their time to have the associational meeting.

Alice Stevens jumped to her feet. "I can't stand this dirty auditorium another whole year!"

Everyone turned to look at her and Nathan rapped on the table. It was difficult to recognize the proper speaker among the several who were signaling a desire for the floor.

Henry Buchanan caught his eye and spoke out, "Anybody can see the roof has to come first. If we don't fix the roof the next rain is going to drop some plaster."

"Well, let's do the roof *and* the painting," Kenny Beck called from his seat, without bothering to get recognition from the moderator.

Rena looked back over her shoulder at him and he slid behind the person in front of him and out of her view.

Ashley rose slowly and waited patiently until Nathan recognized him. "I tell you it ain't possible to do both, but I'll be glad to give you a bid on fixing the roof. I got some men free now could get right on it."

Buck jumped up, face red, eyes flashing. "I will never vote to fix the roof unless it's agreed we paint this auditorium too!"

Old Dr. Davison stood up. He smiled around a little bit before speaking. "I don't know what you're discussing, but I hope you'll save time to talk about painting the sanctuary."

Nathan rapped again for order. The teenagers sitting together on the back pew leaned on each other giggling. Buck and Kenny had their heads together and Al Marceau leaned forward to hear their conversation.

Joe Ponder got up slowly and Myrtle sitting beside him looked anxious. Joe was a mechanic at the Chevrolet garage. His square face was as plain and strong as if drawn by a child with a crayon — black hair straight across the top, fierce black eyebrows, and as if to match, always a trim of black somewhere else about him — thin rims under his close clipped nails, a smudge of oil on his shirt or on the back of his short neck.

He spoke with some heat in his voice. "Now I reckon I'm as careful of money as the next fellow, but I'm getting pretty tired of the stingy and unbusiness-like way this church does things. Brother Moderator, I move we get bids from a couple of painters, and," he paused and looked over at Ashley's ridged head, "and a couple of builders. Then we'll know where we are."

"Second the motion," Buck called loudly.

Samuel Petrie rose to his feet for the first time. Nathan was surprised. Even in deacon's meetings Sam was parsimonious with his words and he seldom took part at all in any conversational group of which Rena was a part. It was as if somewhere along the line he had conceded in advance any territory she chose to occupy.

In spite of the sparsity of his words, or maybe because of it, Nathan had learned that what he said carried weight.

"Mr. Ponder's motion has some merit," he observed quietly, "but I must point out that it is out of order. I believe young Mr. Stevens made a motion some time ago which was not seconded. The ensuing discussion is hence also out of order. The original motion on the matter must be acted upon."

Nathan blushed. Stuttering a little he acknowledged the correction and asked Laura to read the original motion, which was to paint the auditorium.

"Now do we have a second?" he asked briskly, hoping to sound efficient. The first moment of silence stretched into two and then three. Buck reddened and still there was no second. Nathan had no choice. "If there's not a second, then the motion dies." He looked hopefully at Joe Ponder. "Is there a new motion?" Joe sat rooted and silent, his arms folded, his jaw set. Kenny Beck nudged him but he shook his head.

Nathan stifled his own need to blast out at the whole bunch. He could not believe that the only result of all that ridiculous confusion had been to kill the possibility of painting the church. He wound up the meeting not bothering to try to hide his anger.

After the meeting the women clustered in little groups, talking, and the men went out to the sidewalk, muttering and complaining together. Nathan left the auditorium and headed for his study.

Buck caught him at the door. "Sorry, Preacher. We tried. It looks like it'll take an act of God to get this church painted."

"At least," Nathan said.

In his study Nathan sank into his creaking swivel chair and glowered at his desk. Like everything else in the church it was old, beat up. No amount of liquid scratch cover, no careful arrangement of his brass appointments could hide all its scars. One of them was a deep dent the size of a quarter, or the head of a hammer. He slapped his Bible down on top of it.

What the thunder had he gotten into? What a crummy bunch of Baptists. He didn't mind beginning with a small church, but a small-minded church, that was something else again. He'd never get them to move off dead center. They'd never go anywhere, be anything but a limited congregation in a limited building. And they'd limit him in the process.

He swiveled and opened the window behind his desk to let in the cooling air. Leaning back in his chair he took a short, deep breath.

Well, I don't have to stay forever in this situation. If they won't move I will. The first decent opportunity I have I'm going, man, I mean I'm leaving!

There was a sharp rap on his door. He muttered an inhospitable, "Come in," and was not glad to see Rena open the door.

Half standing he asked her to sit down. She ignored the chair by the desk and stood, the fingers of her hand straight and stiff on the top of the desk, her large pocket book held as some men carry a Bible, tight across her breast.

"Can I help you. Mrs. Petrie?"

She snorted. "It's not I who needs help, except to the degree that I'm a member of this church. It's the church that needs help."

Nathan was surprised to find Rena sharing a belief with him.

"I've never seen this church at such a low spiritual ebb. I've never felt such a lack of spiritual fervor or seen so little prayer." She paused. "There's some would say we did wrong to call a young, inexperienced preacher."

"Well, now, Mrs. Petrie," Nathan tried to interrupt.

"I said, 'some,'" Rena continued, "and I didn't say I agreed, because I don't, not altogether."

She sat down abruptly, laid her pocket book across her lap and folded her arms across her breast. "Sit down, Reverend Waite, I've said this much. I'm going to say more."

There was nothing for him to do but sit and he did, taut in his irritation, not only at what she had said, but at the way she was maneuvering the conference.

"There's a sickness in the church caused by unconfessed and unrepented sin."

Nathan raised his eyebrows.

"You know very well what I'm talking about, Rev. Waite. Bill Thompson has been estranged from his wife more than two months because of his sin, yet you have not seen fit to rebuke him. He brazenly comes to church as if nothing had happened, putting his poor wife to continued shame. And that other woman, that adulteress, goes free as a bird, laughing and mocking us all."

Nathan watched her, transfixed. Her black eyes shone, her fingers gripped the edge of the desk as she leaned forward. The light in the study seemed to dim and behind his head a sudden draft of air through the palmetto outside his window carried the wild laugh of the temptress mocking him, the helpless pastor.

36   He moved his chair back suddenly and pivoting around slammed the window shut. Swinging back to face her he was in control of reality.

Looking at her steadily he said, "Mrs. Petrie, exactly what is it that you think I ought to do?"

"To start with you can ask that woman where you live who the adulteress is. She's known from the first and she calls herself a Christian."

Nathan closed a book or two on his desk, put a pencil in the drawer and straightened the blotter. "Nothing I've seen indicates that the woman where I live is anything other than a Christian. It's up to her and the Lord what she does with whatever information she has."

Rena stood up. "You make me sick. You and Cora and that Eleanor too."

Nathan felt extremely tired, too tired for further anger. He picked up the books he wanted to carry home.

"You're right about one thing, Mrs. Petrie. I am a young man and inexperienced, but I can't take credit for all that's wrong with this church. We'd better close shop for tonight. Isn't Mr. Petrie waiting for you?"

5

NATHAN CAME DOWN to breakfast late the next morning. Cora was in the kitchen drinking coffee. When she poured him a cup he sat looking at her without expression, thinking.

"You down at the mouth?" she asked.

"Oh, no," he said sarcastically, "not a whit."

"I don't wonder. Coming home from church last night I told El'na it must be awful trying for a young preacher to have to conduct a meeting like that one."

"Humph." The meeting had been a minor skirmish, she should have seen the battle.

"Rena's already called this morning. I think she thinks you sleep too late."

"No doubt. She's collecting grievances against me."

"Well, I wouldn't know about that, but I do think you'd ought to do something to try and please her."

"Yeah," he said, "like drowning myself in the Oclonee River."

She put her hands on her hips. "Now, preacher, what kind of a way is that for you to talk?"

He sighed. "Okay, okay, but could we just not louse up the day by starting it with Rena?"

"Well, there's something else. Annie Reeves wanted to see you after church, but she said you went so fast to the study . . ."

"I've already visited her son-in-law. I can tell you that Johnny Wilkinson has no intention of coming to our church, nor to any other that I could determine."

His visit with Johnny had not been pleasant. Johnny had been much more interested in loading a seine on the back of his pick-up truck than in talking to Nathan. He had explained that the mullet were running and when Nathan had continued to stand by the truck Johnny had simply gotten into it and driven away. Nathan had absolutely no plans to approach him again.

"This wasn't about Johnny," Cora said. "She wants you to come by to see Worth Parker."

"The paralytic?"

Cora nodded, her eyes round and her face solemn. "Worth Parker is the only atheist in Oclonee. Of course, his father was born a Republican but he never said he don't believe in God!"

"Heaven forbid," Nathan said, and then, "I thought Worth wouldn't let any preacher come near him."

"That's right, but Annie thinks that you being a young man like he is, you might reach him. She's the only one Mr. Parker can get to stay with him, y'know. He's awful hard to take care of — lies up in bed so crippled he can't move his arms or legs, and just can move his head — curses and profanes the name of his Maker all day long. He run off I don't know how many nurses when he first come home. He broke his back in a boat accident at college, y'know."

She shook her head sorrowfully. "The different members of the church have tried to help out, but he won't let them near him. He cursed Rena something awful the day she tried to take him roses from her yard. She came away shaking like a leaf."

"He must be formidable indeed."

"What'd you say?"

Nathan rose. "Oh, nothing." He stood there a minute with his hands in his pockets, thinking. Mr. Parker was at best a nominal member of his church. He was a widower, and one of the wealthiest men in town, living with Worth in a square white house with wide galleries across the front.

Nathan jingled the change in his pocket. He could use a man with Parker's wealth and influence. The Lord knew he needed a few more friendly voices among the older people.

He looked at Cora. "I'll be glad to call on Worth," he said. "I'm going over to the church now. Thanks for the coffee."

He had just settled down at his desk when there was a light tap at his door. When he opened the door he found almost the last person he wanted to see. Pauline stood there acting as if she might run at any sudden move he made.

"Won't you come in?" he asked.

She nodded and stepped past him, looking around the room as if fearful someone else might lurk there. She wouldn't sit down and she scarcely raised her head to speak to him.

"I know you must be upset with Mama," she said.

That's the understatement of the year, he thought, but said nothing. Mama had evidently told daughter about her visit.

"Mama's bossy sometimes, and she can be very hard to please."

That'll do for a beginning, he thought, but he said, "You don't have to worry about it," trying to put kindness in his voice.

"But I do, your being new and all. I guess I want to kind of apologize for her." She looked up, and for a moment there was spirit in her voice, "but if you tell, I'll deny it."

She turned her face to stare out the window. "I had a dog once when I was little. Mama didn't want me to have it, but I begged and begged and Papa thought it would be good for me to have it, being as I was too shy to breathe, hardly. Mama finally gave in, but it just didn't work out at all. Every day that dog did something new to aggravate her, digging up her rose bushes, messing up the porch. . . . She would get furious and carry on so that I'd cry, and then she'd get madder, because I was a cry baby.

"One day the little dog got lost. Every minute I was out of school I walked up and down the sidewalk calling for the dog. Late afternoon of the second day Mama started walking with me and calling and we'd get in the car and drive to other parts of town and get out and walk some more. She started wiping her eyes and blowing her nose . . . said she had caught an awful cold being out in the weather.

"We never did find my little dog, but when I think of me and Mama walking and calling I remember it as one of the best times of my life."

40 Nathan smiled at the girl who was actually looking full at him. "Because you found out she really liked your dog."

Pauline smiled back. "Yes, that, but that wasn't the important thing. The important thing I found out was that Mama could be a cry baby too."

Nathan didn't know what to say. He cleared his throat and made an effort toward the right words. "I appreciate your telling me this, Pauline."

She nodded. "I never told it to anyone else, but . . ." She faltered, looked around and started backing toward the door. "I'd best be going. Kenny will come in for his dinner and wonder where on earth I am."

After she left, Nathan sat drumming his fingers on his desk. *Well, whether or not the old girl has got a soft side,* he reasoned, *I sure have to work with her.* He began to straighten his desk. *I believe, under the circumstances, such a process might be called gumming crow.*

That afternoon as Nathan was leaving the house to make calls Eleanor came in from school. They met in the hall.

"Whither bound?" she asked, smiling her shy smile.

"Worth Parker first."

She looked at him, suddenly serious over her books. "You do know about Worth?"

"That he claims to be an atheist, yes."

"And that he curses like seven sailors at anyone connected with the church."

"Yes, I know. He certainly needs a call from a minister, wouldn't you say?"

"Of course, but . . ."

"Don't worry. If Annie can tolerate him I can. Besides, he's an educated young man and it probably would do him good to have another man with a good education around. We might even strike up a friendship."

Nathan was annoyed at the doubt on Eleanor's face and the slow way she walked up the stairs carrying her books.

Annie met him at the Parker's front door and formed a "shhh," with her lips as she let him in. He stood in the wide dark entry hall, feeling uneasy in spite of himself.

Annie was a thin bird of a woman with eyes the color of old copper pennies. "Thank you for coming," she whispered, and patted his arm. "Before we go in to see Mr. Worth I want to tell you how much I appreciate your going by to see Johnny and Annelle. They're my cross, Brother Waite. I tried to raise Annelle right and you don't know how it grieves me that she's never joined the church. After she married Johnny she just about quit coming to church at all."

A shout from across the hall interrupted her.

"Come back here and shut that blasted door!"

Annie smiled at Nathan. "Worth's got right good strength in his lungs."

"That he has," Nathan said.

Annie patted his arm again. "Don't let him get your goat, or hurt your feelings, no matter what he says. He needs the Lord, and we're just bound to help him see that."

Nathan put his square brown hand over her thin brown one and let her lead him back to the room where Worth lay in his narrow hospital bed.

"Mr. Worth, here's a visitor. I asked him to come. He's our new preacher at First Baptist."

Nathan waited uncertainly for Worth to look in his direction, and after a moment he did. His black hair, streaked with gray, accented the creamy pallor of his skin. His eyes, set deep in his thin face, were black as a moonless night. He stared squarely at Nathan a moment, then laughed and looked away.

"Annie, old girl, you're getting batty in your old age. First you tell me you hear God talking to you and now you're seeing preachers."

Annie moved to the foot of his bed scolding gently. "Why, Mr. Worth. You know you see Brother Waite."

Again the deep blue eyes looked into Nathan's. "Annie, I don't see a blessed thing. Close the door, it's drafty in here." He turned his face to the window.

Nathan touched Annie's arm. "Come on, Mrs. Reeves. It's all right. I'll come again another time."

He didn't make any other calls that day. He went instead to his study where he tried working on a sermon. Giving that up a little later he went home.

42

Eleanor was standing in the dining room door when he came into the house. "Did you see Worth?" she asked.

"Yes." He hung his coat on the hall tree and headed up the stairs.

Eleanor came out into the hall. "Brother Waite?" she said, and when he stopped to look at her from the steps, "Did he curse you?"

Nathan thumped his hand on the stair rail. "Effectively," he said.

6

AN UNEXPECTED WAY to placate Rena occurred the following week when the first hurricane of the season moved up the eastern coast of Florida threatening the beaches as far north as Savannah.

Nathan was sitting in his study watching the palmetto tree outside his window tossing in an erratic wind when an officer of the Coast Guard station called to ask if First Baptist could offer refuge to a group of evacuees from the beach. By a quick call to Sam Petrie Nathan ascertained this was in order.

"It will take some organizing, of course. Plans must be made to collect beds, food, camping stoves and the like. You will probably want to ask one woman to do the basic arranging. The others will pitch in and help."

Hanging up the phone Nathan had in mind a very good basic arranger.

Rena greeted him coolly, but she did greet him, holding her front door open against the wind which was beginning to gust sharply.

"I'm afraid we're in for it," Nathan said, bracing his back against the door to keep it from slamming behind him.

This was his second time in the spotless house and he was struck for the second time with the awesome rigidity of the decor. As he took the place she had indicated she sat down stiffly on the edge of her red velvet chair and focused her black eyes on his.

The wind rattled the tall, narrow windows of the room and Nathan felt the draft of air coming in around the framing.

"I'm sure you are ready for the big blow," he said. "I confess I am somewhat rattled by my first hurricane."

She sniffed. "There's no need to get hysterical, one must simply rest in his faith."

Nathan hadn't thought of getting hysterical, but he let it pass. He was about to go fishing for one Rena Petrie.

"Mrs. Petrie, your experience and calm faith prompt me to ask a very great favor of you."

Rena's face showed an almost imperceptible amount of interest.

Nathan inched forward. "The Coast Guard has asked our church to care for a group of evacuees from the beach, and I'm in a spot. You see, I've never done this sort of thing before, and I need a really dependable person to oversee all the arrangements. I'm wondering if you would consider taking this important responsibility?"

Rena smiled her strange near smile. She cast her eyes toward the ceiling and pursed her lips as if in some doubt — but willing to give the matter grave consideration.

Nathan added bait to the dangling hook. "I'd thought of Cora."

"I'll do it," Rena said.

Nathan slapped his knees and got up. "That's wonderful, just wonderful, Mrs. Petrie. I'm greatly relieved." He paused, getting ready to set the hook. "As to this other problem involving Bill Thompson, I wonder if you and I might not enter into a private prayer convenant that the dreadful affair will all work out to the church's best good."

Rena breathed out a deep sigh and clasped his hand firmly. She was caught.

The next morning Buck talked Nathan into riding to the beach to see how the storm was progressing.

The color of the day was gray — gray sky, gray rain, and when they got to the beach a roaring gray ocean, charging high against the dunes, washing up under the houses. The wind carried the ocean's foam like snow through the air and gusting fiercely moved the car beneath them like it would be the next thing to fly.

"I have a sudden and compelling need to go back to Oclonee," Nathan said, "or maybe to south Georgia." Buck laughed and turning the car headed back toward Oclonee.

At the church Rena ruled happily over what appeared to be a sort of impromptu house party. She was everywhere at once, emitting a steady stream of directions, where to sit, where to play, where to make bunks, what to serve and, absolutely — no smoking.

As the day and the strength of the storm progressed Nathan kept busy, trying to exude an air of geniality and confidence among the Pentecostals, Presbyterians and Episcopalians suddenly in his care. It wasn't easy.

The squalling wind, the torrential rains, the debris hitting the windows had unsheathed his nerves. He could not escape the feeling that something disastrous was impending. By four o'clock the electric lines were down and the candles set high to escape children's fingers cast moving shadows into dark corners. Nathan wandered uneasily into the kitchen where Rena promptly sat him down to cake and coffee. She was on her way upstairs to take a plate of sweets to a group who had gone seeking a quiet place to talk.

In short order she was back, the plate of sweets still in her hand.

"Reverend Waite!" she exclaimed, her voice ringing with indignation, and Nathan felt both alarmed and unaccountably guilty. "What is it?" he stammered.

"The Episcopalians!"

"The Episcopalians?"

"They're playing Bridge in your study!"

Disaster had struck its first blow, but Nathan wasn't sure whether at him or the Episcopalians.

As soon as supper was cooked Rena and her crew left. She had delegated responsibilities for serving and cleaning up among the evacuees. Nathan thought it was a little pointed that she assigned the Episcopalian ladies to wash the dishes.

Bedtime came late at the church. The children, fretful in strange surroundings, reluctantly gave up to sleep, and when they had at last fallen quiet the adults seemed to take on new life, needing more coffee, more talk.

The wind screamed around the church like a beleaguering banshee and in the vortex the old church shuddered. Excursions out into the wind stopped and its encircling howls cocooned the refugees in a warm cameraderie no one wanted to rupture by going to bed.

Nathan finally called time on them at 2:00 A.M. and went to his study leaving Buck to bunk in the basement in case of emergencies. He was stretching his legs under his covers, trying for a comfortable position on the hard curve of the couch's seat when a gathering noise like the fierce ripping of cloth brought him back to his feet.

This is it! he thought wildly, and as he did a horrendous crash echoed and reechoed through the church.

Nathan leaped through the door of his study just as Buck came tearing up the stairs followed by men, women and children coming from all directions and in all stages of dress. Some held flashlights — some candles.

"Put out those candles or we'll have somebody afire," Buck yelled, "and pipe down, will you!"

As they quieted Nathan heard for sure what he thought he had heard. The hurricane had invaded the sanctuary.

He and Buck headed for the sanctuary door, the rest of the crowd following. They were stopped just inside the door by a deluge of rain pouring in from the ceiling.

"The roof must be gone!" Buck shouted.

Nathan anxiously ran the beam of his flashlight up and down the streams of water pouring from the ceiling.

"Lord, help us," he exclaimed without reverence. At that moment the flow perceptibly diminished to thin streams and all but stopped. The rain was over for the moment.

The men by him laughed. "You've got influence in high places," one quipped.

Now Nathan could get a better look. There appeared to be just one very large place in the ceiling from which the plaster had fallen. There was no way to tell what had happened to the roof. Nathan ran the beam of light from one side of the ceiling to the other looking for other places threatening to fall.

"I don't see nothing up there but dirt," Buck said.

Nathan looked at him with real cheerfulness, realizing for the first time what possibilities lurked in the mess of plaster at their feet.

"Ol' buddy," he said, "we might just have had our Act of God."

47

On Friday night Nathan and Buck sat in front of the fire in Buck's den working on a plan.

The church constitution stated that a special business meeting could be called only with the minimum of a week's notice to the church. They figured that on Sunday Samuel would announce a business session for Sunday week in order to get right on with the repair of the church.

Buck would get Kenny and some others to help him call everybody who had ever expressed an interest in redecorating the sanctuary and alert them to the importance of the meeting. Even though the necessity of painting now seemed obvious, Buck was going to take no chances.

"We won't call anybody we're not sure of," he said. "We want to keep it as quiet as possible."

"Yeah, Buck," Nathan said, "if the other side gets wind of it they might try to stack the meeting."

Alice, coming in with coffee, said, "Well, seeing as your big meeting is not until next week you can take me to see about Mother on Sunday."

"Hah!" Buck snorted.

"Hah, yourself," she answered. "I haven't been able to talk to her since the lines went down Thursday. For all I know the storm blew her away."

"There's not a storm running would have the nerve to try," Buck countered.

"Oh, go on and take her," Nathan laughed. "You won't have to be here Sunday. We can get this all lined up next week."

One week later Nathan walked with considerable reluctance toward the brass and marble barn of a building which was Mr. Petrie's bank. He felt exactly like a high school boy summoned to his principal's office, and as angry as he was at his own apprehension he could not get rid of it.

His and Buck's simple little plan to get the sanctuary painted, so simple that it couldn't fail, had failed completely. They had been positive Sam Petrie would call for a business meeting on next Sunday, giving them a week to round up the votes they needed. Instead Sam had called for a meeting of the deacons right after church.

It was all done so easily and quickly, he thought bitterly, by pros. The deacons authorized a full business session after the evening service. When Nathan brought up the article in the constitution saying there had to be a week's notice for such a meeting Mr. Petrie had asked in his perfectly controlled voice if the pastor were not aware of an amendment to the article stating that the deacons could with a 2/3 majority call the church into emergency session.

Nathan scowled. The pastor had not been aware. What could he have done? Buck was gone and he couldn't very well do a Revere act, calling up the right people and shouting, "Business meeting tonight!"

The meeting after church that night was short and to the point. The younger crowd, following their usual pattern, had been slim in attendance, the older crowd coming out in suspiciously large numbers.

Ashley Poole turned up with a stack of neatly mimeographed material showing the church's financial condition, which was not so good. Ashley also brought a statement from a contractor in town, not a member of the church, who said the roof needed extensive repair. He included a bid for the job.

With little argument the church voted to borrow the money to repair the roof and replaster the ceiling of the sanctuary. Ashley then modestly said that he would do the job for a hundred dollars less than the other builder.

His offer was accepted.

Joe Ponder who had tried to raise a little opposition along the way then asked what the church intended to do about the sanctuary other than repairing the plaster. Certainly they didn't plan to leave the white patch like a big eye staring at them from the ceiling.

Few were of the opinion the church should borrow additional funds for redecorating.

Ashley again came to the rescue. Standing in his accustomed place, fingering his emblem, he had looked at the bare lathing and suggested: "Well, now, it seems to me once it's patched, all we need to do is to get a can of ivory paint like the ceiling is already painted, mix in a little soot and cover the new plaster. The whole thing would look the same then."

49

That finished Joe. Red in the face he braced his short arms on the pew ahead of him and shouted, "That is the chinchiest thing I ever heard of, and this has to be the chinchiest church in the whole convention!"

With that he stalked out, leaving Myrtle gasping in her place. And that had been that.

Nathan shook off the bad memory as well as he could and tapped at Mr. Petrie's door. When bidden to do so he entered. Mr. Petrie smiled at him, not unkindly, offered his hand and gestured toward a chair.

Mr. Petrie settled back in his own chair looking down at a thin gold pen which he revolved in his fingers. Nathan waited, as most people waited, until Mr. Petrie was ready to speak.

"I regret the recent conflict of opinion concerning the repair and painting of the church," Mr. Petrie said at last. "I regret, though I'm sure you find that hard to believe, that we could not decorate the sanctuary the way you would have liked, and really, the way it should have been done."

Nathan started to speak but was silenced with a look.

"Although it's difficult for the young to believe that the old have anything of value to say, I do have a small amount of advice I hope you'll accept." He paused, revolving the pen again. "As a young man, you have what I consider a rather normal resentment against the powers that be. You will find, however, that in spite of this resentment it is entirely prudent on your part, when you want something very much, to lay your groundwork for action with the very people you most resent."

Mr. Petrie looked at him quietly for a moment and then observed: "You are not, I realize, wholly unaware of this principle."

Nathan colored, thinking of Rena and the assignment he had given her during the hurricane.

Mr. Petrie continued: "There are various ramifications to this basic truth. You could have, for example, ascertained by a little patient conversation with Ashley Poole that he was not being purely perverse when he said on a number of occasions that the church could not afford two major repair projects, and that the really reasonable thing to do was to repair the roof."

"But Mr. Petrie," Nathan started to protest.

Mr. Petrie's face relaxed in a grave smile. "I know, sir, no one can see the roof."

Nathan sat still, convicted; angry that he had been so easily analyzed, but with a grudging admiration for the analyst.

"There's one further comment I'd make at this time," Mr. Petrie said. "I make it only as a suggestion. It would seem to me that a worthy goal for you to strive toward — one which if reached would solve many of our problems — would be to lead this people in giving more generously of themselves and of their substance." He paused and to Nathan's shock, actually grinned. "We are, as Mr. Ponder has said, a very chinchy bunch."

As Nathan, disarmed and confused, grinned back, Mr. Petrie began to move papers on his desk and Nathan judged the interview to be over. He was right. Mr. Petrie stood and Nathan stood with him.

"I appreciate your time, and your advice," Nathan said sincerely.

Mr. Petrie offered his hand. "I want you to know, sir, that my office is always open to you, and I should feel honored if you would, from time to time, talk with me about what is on your mind."

Walking away from the bank Nathan nearly collided with Ashley Poole.

"Well, now," Ashley said, drawing his chin backwards into his collar. "I've just been by to see the church. It don't look bad at all. S. P. is doing a good job of matching the old paint. You know, when he ain't drinking S. P. is the best painter in town."

Nathan sputtered something about an appointment and headed down the sidewalk. He did not trust his self-control.

Putting S. P. on the job had been a final humiliation. The only possible excuse for hiring the town drunk was because he was Joe Ponder's brother-in-law and the deacons wanted to soothe Joe.

Walking too fast for the warm weather Nathan got hot and wanted to take off his coat. It felt damp and increasingly cloying. He wouldn't have been wearing it except that he'd had to go to Mr. Petrie's office. Mr. Petrie!

Nathan snatched off his coat and swung it over his shoulder.

I am not a child. I will not be patronized, and I will not be harnessed!

When he came abreast of the church he started to pass it by, but his curiosity sent him charging up the front steps. He pushed past the swinging door in the vestibule and into the sanctuary just as S. P. Willard came clunking down the scaffolding near the pulpit.

S. P. glanced at him, shifted the wad of tobacco in his mouth and stooped to wipe his paint brush across the edge of a partly filled gallon can.

Seeing the drops of dirty ivory paint running into the can Nathan exploded.

"Blast it, S. P. This is one week you should'a got drunk!"

7

NATHAN WORKED TENSELY at his desk typing the final copy of a sermon he would preach at an associational meeting in Anderson. It was a fairly important occasion since he would be addressing not only messengers from sister churches but state officials from headquarters in Anderson.

Nathan had only superficial acquaintance with the state people but he knew Paul Conyers, the preacher at the big host church, from seminary days when Paul had been a Fellow in one of his classes. Nathan wanted desperately to impress Paul and the state people and at the same time to show his own people that they were dealing carelessly with a young man respected by other churches, a man to be valued.

A noise from behind his chair distracted him and he swiveled to face the window. Josephina Ponder stood outside, nose pressed to the screen.

Nathan frowned. "Josephina, don't you know it's rude to creep up on people like that?"

She grinned. "Brother LeRoy used to give me candy through this window."

"I'll bet he did. So you'd go away."

"Right," she said, matter-of-factly.

Nathan was not in a gracious mood. "Well, I don't have any candy."

"Gum?"

"Nope."

"That's okay," she said, "because I don't want to go away."

Before he could protest she had run around the church and come trotting into his study. She was wearing a faded pair of boy's jeans, and a sweat shirt cut off above the elbows.

She came to stand close to him, leaning on his chair, and Nathan was aware of a faintly oily smell as if she had been

53

working under a car with her daddy. He stared at her, thinking of what a different sort of little girl he'd have when he had a little girl.

"My uncle S. P. give me these jeans," she said proudly, flopping into the chair by his desk.

She sat there looking Nathan over just as he had been looking her over and Nathan got the feeling he wasn't coming off any better with his matched tie and shirt than she had with her jeans.

"Look, Josephina, I'm pretty busy. Don't you need to go home and take a bath or something?"

She shrugged her shoulders and twisted out of the chair. Coming to his desk again she fingered the pencils in his pencil holder and picked up a white card off a stack of cards — prospects for the church. He took it away from her and groaned at the smudge across the top.

"How did you ever get so dirty?"

She looked with surprise at the fronts and backs of her hands. "I don't know, must'a been when me and Wilbur Jamieson was chucking rocks at ol' lady Cooper's house."

He looked at her with something more than disapproval. He knew about Mrs. Cooper. She was a widow living with an only son in almost complete seclusion. She did not receive callers and did all her shopping in Anderson. No one had seen the boy for years. Gossip said he had some kind of a mental problem, and speculation ran all the way from rumors that he was a helpless idiot to those that said he was violently disturbed and had to be kept chained to a bed. He was used as a threat to frighten recalcitrant children.

Apparently he did not frighten Josephina. She looked at Nathan with some defiance.

"Why do you torment that poor woman?" he asked.

"Hah! She's mean, that's why."

"How is she mean?"

Josephina screwed her face into a ferocious sneer. "She throws things at us kids, that's how, books and dishes and pop bottles. And one time she hit Wilbur's dog with a broom and he didn't do nothing but knock over her garbage can."

Her sneer relaxed in curiosity as she bent over to see what

he had been typing. Afraid she would put her grimy hand on his manuscript he shoved her back a little.

"What's that?" she asked.

"My sermon for a special meeting in Anderson."

"Oh. Is it a good one?"

"I think so."

"Ashley Poole says if you could preach as good as you spend money you'd be a good'un."

His hackles rising he sucked in his breath making ready to answer. She was not through.

"Ashley Poole's a stingy gut. Daddy says."

He closed his mouth.

In a moment she was working on his prospect cards again, stacking and restacking them, finger printing them as she went.

Nathan took them away from her. "Josephina, don't you think your mamma is maybe wondering where you are?"

She leaned her elbows on the desk and her face in her hands looking at him. "Brother Waite, do you think I'm a pest?"

He looked at the little pest and then put his elbows on his desk and chin in his hand mocking her stance. He held the pose a moment and then said, "Josephina, you're not a pest, you're a keen little kid."

She sighed mightily, and standing straight said, "I think I'll give you a present."

Reaching down into her pocket she pulled out a walnut sized wad of tar. As he watched she pulled and twisted it in half. Nathan took his half, trying to appear grateful. He had an awful suspicion of what he was expected to do, and his fear was realized when she popped her half into her mouth.

"Chew it," she said. "I just pulled it today."

"From where?" he asked with a glimmer of hope. Maybe she'd stolen it off a tar wagon.

"From the pavement in front of Lester's grocery." She grinned around her chew.

"Ah, Josephina, I think I'll save mine for later."

She stopped her chewing. "You gonna throw it away when I leave?"

"Throw away your present?"

She narrowed her eyes at him and chewed slowly.

Nathan put the black hunk, dull on the outside from much fingering, shiny at the center, in his mouth.

Josephina's face relaxed. Nathan chewed, hoping the Lord would look upon the colony of germs he was disturbing as so many small lions.

There were voices in the side hall. Josephina shifted her wad to one cheek and stepped to the window. Unlatching the screen she swung it out. "Secret getaway hatch," she explained.

She halted in her escape long enough to lean over and tap the sermon in his typewriter.

"Lay 'em in the aisles, preacher."

He latched the screen behind her with a snap. "I intend to," he said.

Nathan drove back from the associational meeting on a foggy day that was cool and gray as old pewter, but his mood couldn't be dampened. He had been well received by a large congregation and afterward enjoyed late night dialogue with Paul. This morning he had found a good barber and bought two new books. The whole bit had been refreshing.

Cora was polishing furniture in the living room when he came in. "You done real good," she said, beaming. "Coming back yesterday me and Myrtle talked about how proud we were."

He smiled. "Well, I appreciate that." He looked around, wondering where Eleanor was. "Anything new here?"

"Picture show burned down this morning," she announced.

"No."

"Had to call the trucks from Anderson." She pursed her lips. "You *know* who was suspected of starting it."

"Not S. P. Willard."

"Yes, but it wasn't him. Josephina alibied him. They was off fishing together."

Cora looked up the stairs and motioned him to come into the living room. She pulled him down a little to talk in his ear. "Buddy's in town doing some business for his mama.

I don't know if El'na knows, but she's been mighty quiet. It looks like she'll never get over him running out on her."

She raised her voice. "Well, since you're going to eat supper here I better get in the kitchen."

"Sounds like a noble plan. Any mail?"

"Oh, yes, there's mail. Something sweet smelling from Atlanta and one letter come from right here in Oclonee. Couldn't help but wonder what it could be."

"Well, Corrie, if you'll bake me some hot biscuit I'll tell you what's in the letter, if I can. The Oclonee letter that is." He lifted the one from Atlanta, took a deep sniff and flicked his eyebrows at Cora.

"Just hope it isn't trouble," she said. "The Oclonee letter."

"Wash your mouth with soap," he called over the bannister as he ran up the steps.

Julia's letter was short but worthwhile. She had enjoyed hearing from him about his exciting new church and she was looking forward to his coming to Atlanta at Christmas. She was saving some time to get to know him better so he'd better not count on hunting with Turner the whole holiday.

"Little darling," he spoke to the note, "hunting with Turner don't hardly figure in my Christmas plans a'tall."

He folded the letter and put it back in its envelope and the envelope in his coat pocket. He was so far behind in his love life he'd practically forgotten how to take a girl in his arms. He grinned and patted his pocket. He reckoned it would come back to him.

Without enthusiasm he picked up the letter postmarked Oclonee. "Drat you, Corrie," he muttered, feeling uneasy in spite of himself.

The letter was from William Thompson. He was resigning from the Board of Deacons because of Billy's misconduct and continued separation from Effie.

Nathan laid the note down, studying the words without seeing them. *He's not really resigning,* he thought. *He's just making the gesture and hoping I'll turn him down.*

Of course, if the man were serious, then it might be the break he was waiting for. An opening on the Board of Deacons suggested all sorts of possibilities. The letter wasn't

57

necessarily trouble, it might offer instead just a little glimmer of hope.

Nathan collected clean clothes to go take a shower. Walking down the hall he saw Eleanor's closed door and remembered what Cora had said.

He felt he scarcely knew Eleanor though their paths crossed every day — in the hall, at the table, and occasionally in the evening when he was home and sat in the living room a little while with the two women.

At these times he had tried to engage her in something like sustained conversation. She was responsive, but in a detached manner that Nathan had decided was purely self-protective. He could understand that. He had lived in Oclonee long enough to appreciate the shattering blow she must have suffered when Buddy left her, almost at the altar.

He turned the shower on strong and began to lather himself. She was really a pretty thing, he thought, well, maybe not exactly pretty — but she had a certain class with those wide set gray eyes and all that bright hair hanging down her back.

And there was that fragrance she wore — he stopped the motion of the soapy cloth — some perfume he couldn't name. He'd noticed it on occasion when she was near, and a time or two when he had come in late at night, he'd stopped a moment in the dark hall because there was that fragrance hanging in the air.

"Steady boy," he said, and stuck his head under the shower.

8

ELEANOR SAT ALONE on the back steps of Cora's house. The sun dropped behind the horizon, but its light lingered, hanging in banks of color against the sky. Starlings swooped and shrieked, taking their final flight through the dusk before settling twittering in the branches of the pecan trees. Across the fences and hedges separating the backyards of the block the muffled clatter of dishes and voices mingled in a supper time symphony.

Eleanor leaned her head against the step rail and watched the lights go on one by one in the houses nearest her. The strong lines of her jaw and her wide mouth began to weaken and blur even as the straight lines of the houses and trees blurred in the deepening dusk. She drew her knees up and buried her face in the cloth of her skirt. Her narrow shoulders contorted and her arms tightened around her knees, enclosing her grief in a vise.

I can't bear it — I can't — she protested soundlessly against the hard bone of her knees, and then as if to answer an unseen speaker — *it doesn't get better, it gets worse, worse.*

Knowing he was in town, just blocks away, yet totally inaccessible. "Oh, Buddy . . ." she whispered, and in the covering darkness allowed the tears to stream down her face a moment before wiping them away with her skirt.

She heard the kitchen door open behind her and a path of light stretched out in front of her across the nearly dark yard. The door closed and she turned her wet face as the preacher spoke.

"Hello, you playing hide and seek?"

She shook her head.

"Aren't you chilly out here?"

She shook her head again.

"You want me to go away?"

"No. Well, it doesn't matter. Do what you like."

He laughed. "Well, I have been more warmly received in my life."

She ducked her head hastily to give her face a quick brush with her skirt as he sat down beside her, and then raised her head looking straight out into the yard.

After a moment he said quietly, "Got the lonelies?"

"I guess."

He crossed his arms across his knees, whistled tunelessly through his teeth and then asked abruptly, "Did you see Buddy today?"

She sucked in her breath sharply at this direct mention of Buddy. "I didn't see him."

"But you know he's here."

She nodded mutely.

"You want to talk about it?"

Eleanor twisted her hands in her lap. She had never talked about it, to anyone. She had never said his name, to anyone.

"I don't think I can ever discuss it," she said.

"Oh, now Eleanor, that's unrealistic." She turned her head away but he persisted. "Come on now, Eleanor. You can't nurse a brood forever for this guy. It's not right, he's married, and you're too young, and too pretty." He paused, "You are pretty, you know."

She shook her head, looking at him. How could she make him understand?

"You just don't know how it is," she said. "I have always loved Buddy Warren. He was more than just a part of my life. I don't think I can explain it, but it was as if he were me and I him. I thought . . . I know . . . that's the way it was with him too. I don't know, I can't think when it changed. I never suspected any change."

She felt her eyes brim and Nathan put out his hand to stop her, but she couldn't stop.

"He's still a part of me except that now I carry him around inside like a square box with sharp corners, a box that crowds my chest and corners that cut no matter how I turn."

He reached out and took her hand and his hand was warm and strong around hers. When he laced his fingers with hers she held them tight.

They sat that way, without words, in the quiet dark of the evening until they heard Cora calling them to supper.

After supper Nathan showed Cora William Thompson's letter of resignation. She read it and shook her head. "You can't let him do this. It would just kill him. The church has been his life since Lorna died, the church and Billy."

Nathan took the letter from her. "Don't worry, I'll try to get him to reconsider, but if he insists on resigning I'm thinking of trying to get one of the younger men in his place. I'm thinking of Buck Stevens."

Cora put her hands on her hips and frowned. "Buck's the last man for you to push for that job." She pursed her lips speculating. "If you have to get a new man, Durwood Thigpen would be good."

Now Nathan frowned. Durwood was a little bit of a man with hair, skin and eyes all of the same beige color. He entered any room hesitatingly and faded into the wall boards as soon as possible thereafter.

"Durwood is a nonentity," he said ungraciously.

"Well, if you mean he's kind of neutral, that's why I suggested him." She gave him a hard look. "Preacher, there's no need for you to hunt up trouble."

Nathan sighed. "Well, I'll have to go out and see William tomorrow. I'd like to know who upset him anyway. Has Rena gotten busy on this again?"

"Not as I know of. A'course the way she stalks around with that accusin' frown on her face makes everybody feel like they been in the communion crackers."

Mr. Thompson came to his front door wiping his hands on a huck towel. "Come in, Preacher," he said, bowing a little, nervous and uncertain. "Have a seat. Let me just go turn down the stove. I'm making pilaf."

Nathan looked around the room — seasoned old furniture — a framed picture of a sweet faced woman and another beside it of a tow-headed boy in a cotton sunsuit.

When William came back Nathan spoke immediately of the reason for his call. "Mr. Thompson, I appreciate the concern expressed in your note, but I don't feel there is any reason for you to resign."

William shifted in his seat. "Well, I thank you for saying that, but I have been studying about it a lot lately and I just feel it's the right thing to do."

Nathan looked thoughtfully at the unobtrusive man sitting on the couch, a small man with a large problem. Cora was probably right. To lose his position at the church would add knee-buckling weight. Anyway, if he was going to have trouble getting the replacement he wanted he might be better off with this pliable man.

"Mr. Thompson, children of the best of parents can get into trouble. I know you and your wife raised Bill right, and you shouldn't blame yourself now for what has happened, and certainly people who know you shouldn't."

William looked over at the framed pictures on the table. "My wife raised that boy in the hollow of her hand. Soft and gentle she was with him, and he never needed no other kind of raising. If she'd a'lived she'd know what to do now. If she'd a'lived this might not have happened."

They looked up as the front door opened and Bill came in. He stood in the door hesitatingly, seeing Nathan, as if he thought he might be intruding. His father said, "Come on in, son, you know the preacher."

Bill came in to shake hands and William got up. "You all visit and I'll get supper finished. Preacher, will you stay for pilaf? It's my specialty."

Nathan told him Corrie was expecting him and William went back to the kitchen.

Bill sat down near Nathan. "Today is my folks' anniversary, or would have been. That's why dad's cooking the shrimp. The only time he ever cooked when Mamma was living was to make pilaf for her. He can't get over missing her, y'know."

Nathan nodded. "I'm sorry. Bill, did you know he wrote to me saying he wanted to resign as deacon?"

Bill nodded that he did.

62   "Do you know why — I mean why just now?"

Bill shrugged his shoulders. "I think the church folks have given him the business ever since I jumped the tracks. Not anything outright that I know of, but, well, you know there are ways of needling without saying the words."

"I know."

"And I expect he's been especially depressed the last few days with his anniversary coming on. He feels so helpless against his grief. The letter gave him something to do."

"Your father's resigning will not solve your problem, you know that, Bill."

"I know it. I been knowing it. You tell me what will solve it."

"Well, the most obvious thing is for you and Effie to patch things up."

Bill laughed. "Spoken like a single man."

Nathan bridled. "Well, isn't it?"

"Well, preacher, yes it is, and the dear Lord knows I'm willing to be patched to Effie or her to me, but the lady is not willing."

"Have you talked to her?"

"I've tried. She won't come to the door and she won't come to the phone. The last time I went over to Lester's her mama and her daddy both came to the door and told me not to come again. They said I'd hurt her enough and to let her be. I see her sometimes on the street and I see her at the church, but with the whole town watching I can't get up much of a reconciliation speech."

"Bill, Effie's hurt. It takes time for hurt to heal."

"You know what, preacher? I think Effie's madder than she is hurt. She's mad because I wouldn't tell her who I was in love . . . involved with." He looked at the picture of his mother and back to Nathan. "And I'm not going to tell, ever," he said with simple determination.

William Thompson came in and Nathan rose to go.

"Now Mr. Thompson, I want you to forget about resigning your post at the church. From everything I've ever heard you've been a good deacon, and I'd like to have you stay on and give me your backing." He gave his hand a firm shake.

William smiled so gratefully Nathan felt ashamed for a moment. Only a moment. "It's been good to have this little visit. Good to see you, Bill." He gave them both a wave and left, pulling the door shut behind him.

63

Several days later Cora stopped him on his way upstairs. "Preacher, I have to tell you something. Effie's folks are put out with you."

"The Lesters?" Nathan came back down the stairs.

"They know you went to William's house and persuaded him to stay on as deacon."

"How'd they know?"

"I couldn't say. I didn't tell a soul except Myrtle and she promised not to tell."

Nathan folded his lips in and glowered at her.

Cora threw up her hands. "I can't help it if Myrtle is such a gossip. Anyway, they were already a little upset with you because you let Billy help paint the Sunday school chairs."

"That's ridiculous."

"It may be, but that's the way folks are."

Nathan leaned far over the bannister scowling in her face. "How are folks, Corrie, will you please tell me? I don't seem to know."

She backed up a step and folded her hands in her apron. "Well, it's only natural. The Lesters felt like you letting Billy work at the church and then going over and keeping William on as deacon was siding with them, or at least saying you didn't think Billy had done wrong."

"You think that's a natural reaction?"

"I should'a thought of it before you went to William."

"Well, you didn't think of it. You told me to try to get him to stay on as deacon. I was going to take him up on the resignation. Have you decided now I should have let him go?"

Cora let her apron drop in exasperation. "No, preacher, of course you shouldn't have let William go, but you should have gone to Lester's first, give 'em a little sympathy in their trouble, and then gone to William."

He just looked at her.

"Now you'll still have to go, but it'll be harder."

Nathan turned in disgust to go back up the stairs and then turned back to her. "Well, I've got news for you. I'm not going to the Lesters."

64   He took a couple of steps and looked back. She was watching him, twisting the wedding bands on her hand.

He stuck out his jaw. "I am not going."

Effie was the only one at home when he rang the Lester's bell.

She had been cleaning house she said, but she did not look it. She was wearing a dyed-to-match skirt and sweater, an organdy apron with a ruffle and high heels. She took off the apron, clicked back to the kitchen to hang it up, and back up the hall to rejoin him in the living room.

She didn't seem particularly upset with him, but rather sat appraising him coolly as if he were a person that didn't matter to her one way or the other.

"Your folks are at the store I guess," he said.

"They're almost always at the store. They keep longer hours than the supermarket to convenience the customers."

"I imagine they have a good trade."

"They have a good trade."

That finished that subject. Nathan wished Effie had a baby so he could ask about the formula and tooth production. That sort of thing kept conversation alive for hours with young mothers. Effie didn't have a baby. She just had Bill. Well, she didn't quite have Bill either and Nathan had begun to believe that he personally wasn't going to have any peace until this couple got back together.

"I saw Bill the other day," he said.

She raised narrowly plucked brows and swung her foot.

"Effie, Bill would like a reconciliation."

"Hah."

"Why don't you let him talk with you, work this thing out?"

"Bill had plenty of time to talk, but nothing to say."

"Didn't he tell you he was sorry?"

"He was sorry, sorry he had got caught and sorry for that witch he got caught with."

"Well, Effie, Bill seems sincerely concerned with what would happen to the girl if she were found out. I think that's sort of gentlemanly in a way."

She stopped swinging her foot. "And what about me? I'm his wife. Isn't there some gentlemanly sort of way he should think about me?"

Nathan sighed. "Effie, I'm sorry. I expressed myself badly."

She tossed her head. "Oh, I don't think so. You are simply

saying what you feel. Mother and the others are right. You don't take Bill's actions seriously."

Nathan shifted in his chair. "I do, I do take what Bill did seriously. He takes it even more seriously. Why won't you let him come and talk to you?"

"Brother Waite, Bill has hurt and humiliated me before this whole town, and as long as he insists on protecting that girl I take it, and the town takes it that he cares for her more than he cares for me. Under the circumstances I don't see there is anything for us to talk about."

Nathan sighed. "You may be right, Effie. I won't even try to judge. That's not my place, but it is my place to be concerned about your happiness, and the survival of your marriage. If there's anything I can do, I want to do it."

She smiled a little for the first time, relaxing the tautness in her face. "I know you will, Brother Waite. Why don't you run by the store and speak to my folks? They'd appreciate that."

She handed him his hat. "Papa always donates a lot of things for the Thanksgiving boxes. You might speak to him about that, get his mind off of some other things."

Nathan shook hands with her, smiling, and left. Walking toward the car he thought: *The thing that's most often donated in these parts is advice. It's a good thing I'm so tractable.*

He headed his car for main street and Lester's Grocery.

9

RENA CALLED NATHAN before he had finished breakfast on Thanksgiving morning. She was ready to go over to the church to finish decorating and wanted him to come so they could run through the program a final time. She and Brother LeRoy had worked out the agenda for this service and it had to go the same way every time.

When he came downstairs ready to go over to the church Eleanor was in the dining room arranging red leaves and apples around a pumpkin on the table. She wore faded jeans and her long hair was tied in a pony tail with a velvet ribbon. She looked nothing at all like an old maid school teacher.

As he appraised her silently she stopped in her work. "Something the matter?" she asked.

"Nope," he said. And then without planning he added, "Say, why don't I take you over to Anderson for a flick after the big meal?"

She grinned and then the grin faded. "Oh, that would be great, but I don't think we can."

He was puzzled at first. Was she thinking about the engagement to Julia he had faked when he first moved in?

"Oh, Julia wouldn't mind," he said.

"Well, I wasn't thinking about Julia. I was thinking about the folks here. You know how it is."

"Hmmph. Yes, I know how it is."

It was pretty stupid, that's how it was. If he took Eleanor to a movie eagle eyes would begin to gleam and Rena would do more than gleam. She would suspect dark things going on in the house by the church.

Absolutely nothing was going on and he hadn't meant to start anything with Eleanor, but he hadn't had a date since mid-summer and that set some kind of record for him. He hadn't realized in those free and easy pre-Oclonee days how complicated it would be for him to do a simple thing like date a girl once he was The Preacher.

He put on his coat and spoke grumpily. "Well, I guess I'll go over and see how the ladies are doing at the church."

That he could do. It was a poor substitute.

For the Thanksgiving service the pulpit had been removed from the rostrum. Rena and her committee had massed corn stalks and pumpkins along the walls on either side of the baptismal pool and Rena was now working on a huge arrangement of dried leaves and flowers to stand on the edge of the pool. Gertrude Beck and Alma Warren stood by, handing her things as she asked for them.

Nathan admired the women's handiwork.

Rena answered him. "Well, it's going to be nice if I can just get this central arrangement finished and braced properly. It doesn't want to sit up right," she fussed, trying to settle heavy chrysanthemum stalks firmly in the wooden holder, "and I am determined that it shall."

"If it were leaning against something," Nathan tried to suggest, "like the pulpit, for instance . . . you could put the pulpit back in the center."

"I don't want it in the center. I've always had an arrangement on the edge in front of the pool."

"If it falls during the service it would be kind of bad."

Rena stopped her work to give him a hard look. "It's not going to fall."

"I'm sure it won't," he said hastily.

"This has always been such a happy service," Rena sighed, casting her eyes mournfully heavenward, "but of course, this year, there's this dreadful shadow upon us."

"Will you ladies excuse me?" Nathan asked hastily, not wanting to join that old chorus. "I think I hear someone in my office."

The voices hadn't come from his office. Josephina and Wilbur Jamieson were sitting on the side steps eating peanuts and blithely throwing the hulls on the steps and grass.

Nathan stepped quickly out to join them. "Okay, you guys,

get that mess picked up instantly. Don't you know people are coming here this morning for a service?"

"My mama's not coming," Josephina said, "she's too busy cooking dinner."

"My mama never comes," Wilbur said.

"I don't care if nobody even remotely kin to you is coming, you get those hulls picked up." When they didn't seem to be in a hurry he added, "Mrs. Petrie's inside."

They got right to work, their brown fingers grabbing at the shells like fiddler crabs snatching at bait.

Nathan left Rena still fussing with the main arrangement to go and get dressed. When he got back the other ladies had gone, but Rena was still working, an air of desperation about her. She had completed the arrangement, and it was a thing of beauty, but it sat very uneasily on its ledge.

"Just don't use it," Nathan suggested. "The church looks pretty without it."

She looked at him and he knew the arrangement was somehow of vast importance to her. "Wait a minute," he said and went outside to look around the church.

As he had hoped Wilbur was still hanging around. He was collecting acorns and Nathan had one fleeting thought that Wilbur was probably planning to pick off a few thankful worshipers as they left the church.

He grabbed the surprised boy by the arm and pulled him into the church. "Come on, little buddy, I've got a job for you, an important one. I'll give you a quarter after church if you're a good boy and do what I say."

Still pulling Wilbur, he cut through the toddler class room to get a small chair. Then he pulled Wilbur into the back entry of the baptismal pool.

"Just come on," he said. "It's going to be easy."

Wilbur gasped in horror as he realized where they were going. "You're not going to baptize me?"

Nathan gave him a yank. "Someday, I hope, but not today. See?" He thrust the shrinking boy ahead of him as he turned on the light, "No water."

He opened the curtains and called to Rena. "Look, we've

got it made. Wilbur can stand on the chair and hold the flower base from the back. Nobody will see him."

Rena was startled at first, but soon saw the possibilities of the plan. "That's a perfect idea," she said with great relief.

She looked at her watch and wailed that she had to run to dress. Nathan promised to keep Wilbur in his study until just before the service started and then get the flowers on the ledge and Wilbur behind them.

"Don't worry about a thing," he said.

Rena sighed a thank-you to Nathan and then fixed her eyes on Wilbur. The string thin boy tied himself to Nathan's arm under her glare.

"And if you move, Wilbur Jamieson," she said, "or snicker, or let that box fall, I'll skin you alive right here in church."

"I'll hold 'er tight," Wilbur breathed, holding Nathan.

A good crowd came for the service. Josephina's mama had made it after all and she sat with an amazingly clean Josephina and her husband. Next to Josephina S. P. Willard sat, sober, and as amazingly clean as Josephina.

The people coming had brought generous gifts of food for the disadvantaged in the community. Mr. Lester would add a pork roast to every order before it was delivered.

The Lesters were there and Effie sat beside them, her body half turned so that she would in no wise catch a glimpse of her husband who had come in and was sitting with his own dejected-looking father on the opposite side of the church.

Some of the adults and all of the teenagers on their accustomed place on a back pew behaved like spectators at a ping-pong match, swinging their heads to look first at Effie and then at Bill.

Nathan called a number and they all stood to sing.

"Come ye thankful people, come
Raise the song of harvest home!"

The thing I'll be most thankful for, Nathan thought, *is to have this thing with Effie and Bill settled before Christmas.*

As soon as the service was over Rena steamed into action again, in a hurry to get the baskets delivered. "So the poor dears can have a nice Thanksgiving supper," she explained.

The baskets were put in the back seat of Mr. Lester's pickup truck which Nathan would drive with Kenny beside him to help.

Nearing the end of the task Nathan cut down a back street following Rena. They passed the Wilkinson's small house with its neat beds of marigolds in old black tires. Nathan thought again as he had before, that the fisherman probably wouldn't be happy at First Church anyway, excusing himself for not making an additional call. Down the block in front of them Rena stopped suddenly in front of Jamieson's house.

"Why's she stopping there?" Kenny asked. "The Jamiesons aren't on our list."

Nathan braked so suddenly Kenny was thrown forward. And as Rena turned in the Jamieson's driveway, Nathan backed a little to turn in the Wilkinson's. Nathan just did beat Rena back to the church.

He ran into the sanctuary and up on the rostrum.

Rena's arrangement stood firmly anchored.

Gently parting the curtains in front of the pool Nathan looked over the flowers and down into a distressed brown face. Down each lean cheek a white line ran where tears had streamed through the dirt.

Nathan lifted the arrangement and sat it on the floor. "Oh, my goodness, Wilbur, I'm sorry. Did you think we had forgotten you?"

Wilbur nodded his head mutely.

"Were you scared?"

Again the nod. "And I was gettin' hongry."

Nathan reached in his pocket to see if he had a buck. As he did Rena appeared suddenly at the back door of the baptistry.

Gasping for breath she came clonking across the metal floor of the baptismal pool to swoop Wilbur against her large bosom in a strong embrace.

Wilbur looked at Nathan with something like panic. *I suppose he'd almost rather be baptized,* Nathan thought, hurrying to rescue him.

71

10

ON AN EVENING IN MID-DECEMBER Nathan joined Cora and Eleanor at the dining room table. Cora was finishing doll clothes for the Children's Home Christmas box, Eleanor grading papers.

"Now isn't this peaceful?" he said, opening a manila folder of plans for the Christmas program out on the table. He looked up. "As a matter of fact it's been peaceful around here since Thanksgiving."

From her papers Eleanor observed drily, "Which block of time corresponds roughly with Rena's visit to Brunswick."

Cora looked from one to the other. "Speaking of peace," she said and stopped as if she weren't sure they were. When they laughed she pointedly ignored them and went on. "I was telling El'na before you come in that she ought to go to Miss Alma's Christmas Tea. We both got our invitations today."

"Speaking of peace!" Eleanor cried, throwing up her hands.

"Well, I think Corrie's right, El'na. You ought to go."

"I can't. Sarah Sue and Buddy always spend Christmas at Miss Alma's, and Sarah Sue will be at the tea. We can't meet again for the first time in front of half of Oclonee."

Nathan was astounded. "Have you really not seen her in all this time?"

Eleanor shook her head without looking at him.

"I can't believe it," he said. "Hasn't there been any effort toward a reconciliation?"

Eleanor looked at him now, her eyes flashing. "None whatsoever, unless you call Miss Alma sending me an invitation to her annual tea an effort. They have never come near me or written me a line, not even when the baby was born. I'm not running to them!"

"That's right," Cora said.

"No, but it's about time for both sides to do some running, don't you think?" Eleanor dropped her head again. "Will you let me help?" he asked.

"What can you do?" she asked dully.

He had been thinking. "I can find out from Miss Alma exactly when Buddy and Sarah Sue are coming again and arrange for you to call."

"Nathan, I couldn't!"

"Yes you could. Corrie will go with you or I will if you like. Eleanor?" She wouldn't look up.

"Course she could," Cora bit off a thread with a snap. "El'na's got the gumption to do whatever she knows is right."

Eleanor looked at Cora and then at Nathan. "All right," she said. "It has to come sometime, it might as well be now."

"Good girl," Nathan said. He watched her a moment and then looked down at his own work, thinking about Alma Warren. Nathan had eaten dinner at the wealthy widow's house and had observed then and in the months following that Miss Alma had a place of influence in the town as well as First Baptist. He consciously deferred to her knowing he was guilty of fence building. This was easy to rationalize. He had a very real need for support among the older people in his work at the church. In fact he'd been counseled by Mr. Petrie to seek it.

He tapped his pencil on the list in front of him. A genuine reconciliation between the Warrens and Eleanor was certainly in order and if he could help it along it wouldn't hurt his cause any.

He spoke aloud to Eleanor. "I'll call Miss Alma in the morning, and set up an appointment for you. I think I'll just go along to give you moral support."

When the time came Nathan walked with Eleanor the short distance to the Warren home. Casting an occasional glance at her Nathan saw her take sudden deep breaths and wondered if it were the cold that made her gasp or the anxiety of the moment. Uneasiness rose in him. Was this ordeal he had maneuvered her into really justified? He had meant to be practical, but not callous.

She paused near the Warren's where an entire block of

the cement walk heaved up crazily over the thrusting root of a giant oak tree.

Catching in her breath sharply she said, "Step on a crack, you'll break your mother's back," and Nathan knew she had been caught with a memory.

"Let's skip the whole thing," he said abruptly.

She looked at him, her eyes wet with wind or tears, and shook her head fiercely. A car slowed down, the riders watching them. Swinging her purse Eleanor marched down the sidewalk to turn in at the Warren gate.

Nathan followed her reluctantly up on the porch. Seeing she was determined he stepped ahead of her and turned a key in the brass circle on the door. Inside a bell rang.

Alma Warren answered the door. "Well, here you are," she said with a trembling small voice. "It's good to see you, Brother Waite, and Eleanor, dear." She fussed nervously with the gold brooch pinned at her neck.

"How are you, Miss Alma?" Nathan asked.

"Oh fine, fine. Let me take your coats."

Hanging them in a closet she said, "It's good of you both to come." Coming back to Eleanor she took the girl's hands in hers. "It's especially good to have you here again, Eleanor, I've missed you."

Suddenly tearful she took a finely embroidered handkerchief from the bosom of her dress and dabbed at her eyes.

Keeping Eleanor's hand in hers she led them toward the back parlor. The long entry hall was dark with old mahogany relieved only by the shaft of colored light coming through the stained-glass windows on the stair landing.

Buddy Warren stood up immediately when they came in and Sarah Sue, pregnant, caught his arm and pulled herself up awkwardly. She did not look at them, but up at Buddy.

Nathan hadn't formed a mental image of Buddy, but his actual appearance was an unpleasant surprise. Buddy was an inch or more taller than himself and built like he had played a lot of basketball well. He had heavy brown hair which went off at angles in double cowlicks above his temples, and brown eyes. Nathan thought reluctantly he would have to say "warm" brown eyes.

Thinking to give Eleanor a little more time he stepped

forward to shake hands with Buddy and to speak to Sarah Sue. Stepping back he put one hand firmly against Eleanor's shoulder blades, not at all to push, but to support.

Buddy held out his hand and Eleanor took it, looking up into his face. Nathan dropped his hand from her back and turned away, feeling quick shame to have intruded upon this moment, and a twinge of another emotion he would not name.

He heard Buddy murmur something to Sarah Sue and from the corner of his eye saw Sarah Sue lean forward to touch her cheek to Eleanor's.

"Well, now," Miss Alma said with a great sigh. The dreaded formalities were over.

Nathan turned back to the group, a little uncertain as what ought to be said or done.

"Let's all sit down," Miss Alma said. "I'll have Mamie bring us coffee. Remember Mamie's good little cookies, El'na? You and Buddy . . ."

Buddy frowned. Sarah Sue tugged at his arm. Eleanor said too brightly, "Of course, I remember Mamie's good little cookies. Don't we all?"

They sat awkwardly on the big old chairs, their fingers picking at the linen protectors on the arms. The fire in the grate snapped and they watched the minute diversion eagerly.

A small face popped around the green velvet drape hanging in the arch between the front and back parlors. A small body followed the face as by slow degrees a little boy entered the room. Avoiding his father's outstretched hand he went directly to Eleanor and stood in front of her.

They studied each other, he showing no emotion other than slight interest, she with something like awe on her face.

"Are you Robert Delaney Warren, Jr.?" she asked.

"I Little Buddy," he replied, corking his mouth with his thumb.

He had his father's brown hair and identical cowlicks standing awry on each side of his wide forehead.

"He has father's eyes," Eleanor said.

"And your's," Buddy added.

Sarah Sue spoke for the first time. "Little Buddy looks exactly like his daddy. Everyone says so."

Eleanor nodded, not taking her eyes off the child. Little

Buddy suddenly released his thumb and ran to his father where safely on that lap he re-inserted his thumb.

A general sigh of relief swept the room when Mamie arrived with the coffee. The tiny Negress nodded around the circle, smiling her pleasure at seeing them all. Taking Little Buddy from his father's lap she put him in a chair of his own. She giggled.

"It shore beat all how he favor you, Miss El'na."

"It's the Boyette eyes, Mamie," Eleanor said, coloring.

"Yes'm, Boyette eyes and Boyette mouth. He all Boyette 'cept he hair."

Miss Alma interrupted hastily, "Why don't you bring us a little dish of your candied grapefruit peel, Mamie."

Nathan found Mamie's cookies not all that much to brag about. He got restless in his chair watching Eleanor in a state of near adoration before this square-headed child with the stupid cowlicks.

As soon as he reasonably could he rose and suggested that he and Eleanor ought to go.

Buddy got up as if to see them out, but Sarah Sue caught his arm and held it.

Miss Alma and Little Buddy walked them to the door. Miss Alma kissed Eleanor's cheek and thanked Nathan for coming.

Nathan leaned down to the little boy and asked, "Would you like to shake hands?" Into the mouth went the thumb and behind Miss Alma's skirts went the child.

"I'm glad to have met you, Little Buddy," Eleanor said, peeking around at him, but he would not come out.

She hurried through the door in front of Nathan and he saw her draw her coat tightly around her as if she had grown very cold.

11

THE NIGHT SET FOR THE CHURCH folks to go caroling was mild and moist, a spring bonus in the midst of winter. Pulling on his sweater Nathan looked out the window at the fullish moon and whistled a little non-Christmas tune. He was actually looking forward to the unsophisticated ritual — especially since Eleanor was planning to go — breaking her usual pattern of solitude.

She was waiting in the living room when he came down, wearing a deep blue corduroy jumper and a soft sweater that asked for touching. Opening the door for her Nathan wondered how in the world Buddy could have left her for Sarah Sue. He'd just plain robbed himself.

In the church yard the carolers were gathering, calling greetings and singing snatches of Christmas music. Most of them were teenagers, but there was a good sprinkling of adults standing around self-consciously and a few children chased each other back and forth in patternless joy.

Alberta twittered out a small bit of information. "Durwood isn't coming after all. They're so busy at the Post Office. Christmas rush, y'know."

Or a simple escape, Nathan thought. He nodded at her and reached out to give Buck a fist in the ribs. "Well, I'm glad you decided the Kiwanians could survive without you for one evening."

Kenny Beck jibed, "You didn't think Buck would let Alice gallivant all over town without him?"

Alice made a face at Kenny. "With the preacher I wouldn't be safe?"

"With the preacher you especially wouldn't be safe," Kenny countered and everyone laughed, except Buck.

Nathan exited to the kitchen, vaguely troubled without knowing why.

Agnes Renfroe was standing by the stove looking distraught. She indicated the boxes of doughnuts, cans of milk and cocoa on the table. "People have brought this stuff in but Bessie Poole has the flu and I haven't the vaguest notion how to use this antique stove."

Nathan was disappointed that Bessie couldn't come. He had personally recruited her for the project, trying to soften the Poole's attitude toward him. He hastened to soothe Agnes, afraid she might take off. "Don't worry, I'll get you some help."

Running back out to the yard he corralled the crowd and waved down the noisemakers. "Bessie Poole's got the flu and I need an instant volunteer to take her place in the kitchen."

They looked briefly but not deeply concerned over Bessie's flu. The teenagers knew he couldn't be talking to them and resumed their bugging immediately. Dolly and Alice looked at each other, hesitating and in that moment Eleanor said, "I'll be glad to help Agnes, Brother Waite."

"Not you, Eleanor," he said hastily. "You've got to carol."

Alberta Peeples raised her eyebrows and a couple of the others exchanged glances.

"Nonsense," Eleanor said. "Everybody knows I can make chocolate better than I can sing."

Nathan was caught. They were all watching him. He flailed himself mentally for not calling Cora the instant he'd heard about Bessie. Now he couldn't do it without making an issue of it.

As Eleanor disappeared into the church he clapped his hands together sharply.

"All right, let's get organized. Alberta is going to tell us which carols we will sing and Kenny Beck has the basket of Christmas greens. I'm going to ask Josephina and Adelaide to be responsible for taking a spray to each door where we sing."

The little girls smiled proudly and Alberta trilled her giddy laugh and came to stand by his side. When she had counted off the planned carols on her long, manicured fingers she trilled again and slid her hand under Nathan's arm.

"Come along, group," she called gaily.

Nathan came along after a quick glance at the lighted church basement.

This is not what I had in mind, he thought glumly, but after a moment the humor of the situation caught hold of him. He grinned in the darkness thinking of the other young spinster in the church. Laura Adams should have come. She could have had his other arm.

They sang first at the nearly empty hospital and then they stopped by Worth Parker's house. Nathan had considerable reservation about singing here, but Alberta had insisted it was the Christian thing to do, and he had acceded.

The group formed under Worth's window quietly, the light from his room a spotlight on their center ranks. The middle of his bed was within Nathan's vision, but he could not see Worth's face.

Alberta waved her arm, starting them out.

> "The first No-el the angel did say,
> Was to cer-tain poor shepherds
> in fields as they lay . . ."

They had gotten just to the first chorus when Annie's slight figure appeared at the corner of the window. Giving a surreptitious little wave she slowly closed the drapes.

Nathan faltered along with the rest of the group, but only for a moment. Strengthening his voice he led them to the close of the chorus and then raised his arms hushing them.

"If he doesn't want us to sing," he said quietly, "we won't sing. Perhaps he's had a bad day."

Aunt Sally Lennon was waiting for them. She stood in her open front door leaning on her cane while they sang and when they had finished, shouted them all into the house for homemade divinity, shooing the cats off the chairs for them to sit down.

She was delighted with her spray of greens and made them wait while she found a hammer and nails for Nathan to put it up over the archway into her living room. 79

As he got down off the chair she gave him a tremendous

nudge and shouted to the others, "Too bad there's not some mistletoe in it, aye, girls?"

"Too bad indeed, Aunt Sally," he said as Alberta caught his elbow to lead him off to the Poole's.

Ashley didn't invite them in, but he stood by his front door peeking out the little strip of glass at its side while they sang and he waved his handkerchief at them from the door when Josephina took him a spray of greens.

They started back to the church in high spirits singing over and over, "We wish you a Merry Christmas," and shouting it to any car that passed.

When they approached the almost dark Cooper house standing in ghostly whiteness on its bare corner Nathan had an impulse and stopped them in the middle of a chorus.

"Let's sing for Mrs. Cooper," he said.

Josephina jerked his coat. "Ol' lady Cooper?"

The crowd laughed.

"Why not?" he asked. "She must be very lonely at Christmas."

They looked at one another, and Nathan knew they were probably remembering their reception at Worth Parker's.

"Oh come on, gang," Buck said. "It's Christmas."

"I'm not scared of ol' lady Cooper," Josephina bragged. and without waiting for Alberta to start them planted herself at the front of the group and began in piercing voice,

"The first No-el the angels did say . . ."

Nathan waved to the group and they all joined in, lustily, as if Mrs. Cooper might be hard of hearing.

In a matter of seconds Nathan saw the drape which had been closed at the bay window in the front room move slightly. A hand pushed it aside and someone stood there outlined in the dim light as they sang through their entire repertoire.

When they had finished Josephina snatched at the remaining spray of greens in the basket Adelaide was holding, and marched up to the Cooper front door. She rang the bell and waited.

The drape closed at the window but the door bell went unanswered.

After a moment Josephina shrugged her shoulders, laid the spray in front of the door and came marching back to where they waited.

"It was my turn," Adelaide said crossly.

Josephina shrugged. "Sorry, kid."

Nathan cleared his throat. "Who's for hot chocolate?"

That was all they needed. The kids and teenagers left in a run for the church, the young adults walking more leisurely behind.

Nathan was not alone. He still had Alberta.

Nathan was irritated with Eleanor when she insisted on taking Little Buddy to the Christmas program at the church, but by the time the program was over he had mellowed and offered to walk them home.

It was such a beautifully clear night. He carried the little boy most of the way and by the time they reached the big old white house, spooky in the shadows of the great oaks surrounding it, the child was asleep on his shoulder. He handed him over to Mamie at the door feeling almost paternalistic.

Eleanor hunched her shoulders as they left, raising the collar of her coat higher on her neck against the wet wind blowing cold from the ocean.

Nathan rubbed his hands together and said briskly, "Well, it was a good evening, good program."

Eleanor did not answer at once and when she did her voice had a soft huskiness. "Little Buddy got so involved. He wanted to see the baby Jesus. He thought he was really in the manger."

"Eleanor . . ."

"Hmmm?"

"Eleanor, don't go overboard over that baby."

"What do you mean?"

"Well, you know. You've been through this difficult thing with Buddy and you're just beginning to break through on that, but don't make the mistake of transferring your feeling to that little kid. I don't think that's the solution."

"He's my nephew. He's my only sister's child! Can't I love him?"

"Yes, of course, if it's a normal aunt-nephew love, but don't make him bear a burden that's not his."

"I don't know what you're talking about."

"Oh, come on, Eleanor . . . you're not dumb. That baby's not just your sister's child — he's Buddy's child."

She turned her face away. "Let's don't talk about it anymore."

"Okay." He began to whistle softly.

"Jingle bells, jingle bells . . ."

"Are you excited about going home?" Eleanor asked.

"Hmmm? Oh sure — it'll be great to see the folks again. I'm going to Atlanta, too, after I've been home a couple of days. I'm really looking forward to that." He whistled another bar and then added, "You know Baptist preachers don't go to heaven, they go to Atlanta."

When they had walked a little further she asked, "Are you going there to see Julia?"

He smiled and whistled through his teeth. "Yes, indeed, I will certainly see Miss Julia Harrison."

Eleanor nodded. "I thought you would," she said, and in a moment, "Pretty name."

"Pretty girl," he said.

They walked quickly past the houses, many of them already dark, some with the lights of Christmas trees shining through the windows.

When they came to the church it was dark. The janitor had locked up and gone home. The porch light was on at Cora's house, and her tree glittered against the window panes.

"Race you!" Nathan cried suddenly and they both ran down the sidewalk, up the steps and into the hall, banging the front door behind them.

"For heaven's sake," Cora said, looking down at them from the upstairs hall. She already had on her long, faded robe and her sparse hair hung down over her rounded shoulders in one thin plait. "What'll people think?"

82   "People ought to be in bed," Nathan said, taking Eleanor's coat and his own to the hall tree.

"Well, that's where I'm going. There's cake and coffee in

the kitchen if you're hungry. Nathan, turn off the lights when you come up."

Eleanor brought in crumbly slices of fresh coconut cake and coffee and they sat on the floor in front of the fire. Untended during their absence it had burned to little more than ashes and red coals that snapped occasionally, sending up thin plumes of smoke.

"Isn't it beautiful?" Eleanor sighed.

"Yes, it is," Nathan said, watching the wavering light from the coals tint her face.

"I think," she turned suddenly and catching his intent gaze seemed to forget what she was thinking.

"Would you like more coffee?" she asked instead.

He looked away and at the fire. "No, thank you," he said, "I won't sleep now."

"Christmas time is not for sleeping. I dearly love Christmas and this year for the first time in a long time I think I'm almost happy." She laid her hand on his. "That's partly because of you. You have been a real friend." She looked at him with a trace of wonder on her face. "I never thought a preacher could be a friend, you know what I mean, a friend."

"Yeah, I know what you mean, unfortunately." At her puzzled look he grinned and got to his feet, pulling her up beside him. "Friend or not, it's getting late and Corrie will be hollering down about the lights again in a minute."

Still holding her hand he turned off the lamp. He did not want to let her go. He knew clearly what he wanted to do, but there she stood with that open, "friendly" look on her face, and he hesitated.

"Now if you were an ordinary girl and I an ordinary boy . . ." He hesitated another fatal moment.

Cora's voice came down to them, "Nathan, did you forget the tree lights?"

He sighed. "But I am not an ordinary guy and you are not an ordinary girl." Folding her hand he raised it to his lips for the gentlest whisper of a kiss.

"Goodnight, my little friend, and a Merry Christmas," he said.

12

ON THE LAST DAY of his visit at home Nathan sat in his mother's kitchen listening and trying to give answer to his mother and his three married sisters, feeling a mixture of pleasure and frustration. It was not a new sensation.

As the youngest child and only son in his family he had grown up vacillating between fierce love for the females who dominated his life and a strident need to break away from their supervision.

His father, who could have provided male relief, was seldom at home, not even long enough to farm the small acreage he had inherited. Since the salary he drew as a country preacher was never large enough to buy bread and shoes for his family he worked wherever work was available, in the fields of neighboring farms or, when he was more fortunate, at the county seat feed store. Nathan could still feel resentment remembering that when his father did come home it was often to set him to some hard task on the farm or to administer a licking prescribed by one of the females.

But it had not always been that way. As a very little boy he had both reverenced and adored the big man, running to meet him with impartial joy whether his father came home from the fields in filthy overalls or from some pastoral ministry in his preaching suit.

How many times had he made that joyful run, spotting their old car half a mile down the road from his lookout's perch in the chinaberry tree. He could still feel the damp denim of his father's pants leg against his cheek, and smell the mixture of sweat and earth deep in his nostrils.

How many times had he sat wide-eyed on a front pew listening to his father thunder from the pulpit, sweat staining the preaching suit, the good tie gone as far astray as the sinners in the pews before him. How many times had he stretched out on the pew to sleep in full confidence, knowing the thunder from the pulpit was not for him.

When had he stopped adoring? When had he first felt shame at the work, the sweat, the near illiterate language of his father?

Was it the books he read, the clothes his schoolmates wore, the growing knowledge that there was a better way of life — easier and more fruitful than the one they were living on the farm?

Nathan moved uncomfortably in his chair and looked over at his mother who was knitting with a small frown on her face. She had always made up for her small size with extra energy and was clearly growing irritable over the time they were consuming doing nothing during his visit.

His sister Martha Ann shoved aside a child who had leaned on her too long and rephrased a question he had not answered to her satisfaction. "But Nathan, when are you going to find the right girl? After all, you're twenty-four."

"I don't know," he said, untangling a niece's fingers from his watch band. "I'm working on it."

"Who are you working on, Turner's sister?"

"Well, maybe. I'll know more after I see her tomorrow."

"Oh come on, Nathan," Susie said, "Julia Harrison was a debutante. Even if you did room with her brother she wouldn't give you a second look."

His mother spoke testily. "Just because she was a debutante doesn't make her too good for Nathan."

The conversation ceased while the girls separated the children who had gravitated into a single rolling ball of flying arms and legs.

"Go out and play in the sun while it's warm," their grandmother said and stared them out of the door before resuming her knitting.

The girls took up where they had left off. "What's this Eleanor like?" Betty Faith asked, cutting her eyes over at her mother.

Nathan sighed, resigned to their curiosity. "Eleanor is a real fine girl."

Betty Faith was exasperated. "That isn't what I meant. Is she pretty or smart or musical or anything, except 'real fine'?"

"Now wait a minute," Nathan protested.

"You girls let Nathan be," his mother said. "Let him pick his own wife in his own good time." He was feeling grateful and then she added, "Nathan doesn't have to settle for a small town nobody."

Rising, Nathan faced his mother and the three girls, indignant and defensive. "Eleanor is not a small town nobody. She is sharp, well-educated, and pretty enough for any man."

They looked at one another with smirks and raised eyebrows and he was furious. "Eleanor happens to be carrying a giant sized torch for another guy and she doesn't even see me except as a friend and her pastor. So you can just lay off Eleanor, see?"

His mother had risen hastily, laying her knitting behind her and now came to grip his arms with her small strong hands.

"Now son, don't get put out with us. We're just interested in your welfare. You know that. We want you to be happy in a good marriage."

He patted her hand though he felt very little warmth toward her at the moment. "Like you said, Ma. I'll pick my own girl in my own good time." He turned to go outside and then glared back at his sisters. "And don't be so cotton-picking sure I can't come up with a debutante."

To his relief the nieces and nephews had gone off to the barn to play. He could hear them screaming in some ritual game and from time to time one or two would flash out like low flying birds and back into the barn again. His anger muted itself into loneliness as he walked aimlessly around the winter bared yard coming finally to lean disconsolately against the chinaberry tree.

In the walnut paneled den of the Harrison's home in Atlanta Julia and her brother Turner were waiting for Nathan's arrival. He was coming in on a bus and would call from the station.

Julia idly slid her fingers over a porcelain figurine on a highly polished end table beside her chair. Her perfectly shaped nails had been manicured that afternoon and her fine blonde hair carefully coiffed and lacquered to hold its casual shape through any exigency.

She wore an emerald green velveteen dress and in her ears and around her throat the pearls her father had given her when she graduated from St. Catherine's.

"Nathan's late," Turner remarked, just as the small gold clock on the mantel began to chime the hour of eight.

"How perfectly ridiculous for him to come on the bus," Julia said, feeling both irritated and amused.

"Everyone can't afford the air, Julia, dear."

"Why didn't he drive?"

"If he still has the old wagon from seminary days the bus is a decided improvement. Besides, if you are so disdainful of him and his bus why do you sit here waiting to see him? You could be out with one of your affluent chums who all have spectacular cars."

Julia held out one hand, examining its flawless manicure. "Because they are boring and so are their cars." She added the second hand for scrutiny. "Your Nathan intrigues me."

"My Nathan, before he's through, will intrigue a lot of people. I predict he will be a real big man in our convention one of these days."

"How much could such a man hope to earn?"

Turner laughed. "Not enough to keep you, sweetie pie."

"For such a big man I might be willing to sacrifice a little."

"Are you kidding?"

"Of course."

She got up and went over to the mirror hanging above the fireplace. Turning her head from side to side to let the hair swing gently she thought: *Am I kidding?*

Julia was utterly disinterested in the kind of life she saw developing for her married friends. She didn't want to be a suburban housewife with two cars, two babies and one sloppy maid. She didn't want a husband whose chief passion in life was University of Georgia football.

Julia saw in Nathan the same things Turner saw. He was a little on the unpolished side, but absolutely destined to achieve in his field. And surely, in spite of what Turner said, the wife of a pastor of a really important church could maintain a certain standard.

Her vision of herself in a fastidiously decorated church parlor pouring tea was interrupted rudely by Turner.

"There's one thing that may betray Nathan in his ambitions," Turner said. "He may trip and fall over his shepherd's heart."

Julia turned and raised her eyebrows.

"If you don't know what it means, I'll spare you the explanation."

The telephone rang. "That will be the shepherd," Turner said.

Heading back toward Florida Nathan leaned his head against the clean cotton towel on the back of his bus seat and watched the familiar landscape flash by — empty red fields waiting for early planting, corn fields with broken stalks still standing forlorn against the sky, tenant houses at the end of rutted roads, their windows shuttered against the cold, their chimney's unfurling listless spirals of smoke.

At the edge of the towns the owners of the fields lived in sharply white or antique brick houses. They had low brick walls or boxwood hedges to protect them from the streets and opulent wreaths concocted at florist shops hanging on their brass fixtured doors.

Nathan had just visited behind such a door. Turner had picked him up at the bus station in a new Mercedes and they had gone by to get Turner's fiancee before going back to the Harrison's house. Ann was very like Julia.

Julia. What a vision she was in the green velveteen, and his date for the first evening without his even asking.

"Well Nathan Waite," she'd drawled in soft Atlantaese. "Aren't you the sweetest thing to come and see us again. Did you leave your family well?"

"All right, Scarlet," Turner mocked.

"Whatever are you talking about?" she murmured and tucking her small hand under Nathan's arm led him to a couch fronting the fire and sat beside him, close, her arm linked with his.

"I thought we were going to take Nathan to see the tree at Rich's," Ann said as Turner took her stole.

"It won't run off," Julia said. "Let Nathan warm up a little. It's awful cold outside."

He had warmed up all right, and she had not let his temperature drop during the whole of this visit. But after their last date, when he was telling her good night, neither the open invitation in her manner or his need to accept it kept him from feeling awkward when he took her into his arms.

She turned his awkwardness into grace, moving so lightly against him that he hardly knew when she had come. But he knew she was there and he liked the softness and the scent of her, and when they kissed he forgot entirely that she was Judge Harrison's daughter.

"Man!" Nathan said aloud, remembering, and then looked around self-consciously to see if anyone on the bus had heard. No one had, or if they had it made no difference to them.

He leaned back against the head rest watching shiny blue black chickens scratching in the red clay at the edge of the road.

"Georgia ... Georgia ..." he hummed under his breath.

By late afternoon Nathan was tired of the bus and his memories. The earth had lost its red and from the bus window he watched fields covered with Bermuda grass alternate with low swamps where Cypress trees bogged to their knees in black water and wearily held out arms burdened with Spanish moss.

A loneliness as gray as the moss shrouded his spirits. The Harrison's world of heavy linen and polished silver now seemed remote, but so did the farmhouse of his parents. And he had not been able to get the two worlds together in his mind at all. The frustration of trying had no doubt contributed to his depression — or given him the "bots" as Cora would say.

Corrie. He had really missed the bossy old gal. Always telling him what to do like she knew everything. Telling him what to say — who to go see — and how to treat people. Eleanor for instance. As if she had to tell him how to treat El'na.

Nathan smiled and closed his eyes. *I've missed that shy little critter too,* he thought. *I've missed the solemn dignity she gives to the commonplace and I've missed her gray eyes suddenly gone from solemnity into fun.*

*We always get a joke at the same time. She's really sharp.
You don't have to draw her pictures.*

Nathan opened his eyes as the lights of a filling station flashed by and then more lights as they rolled into a sizeable town. Nathan looked at his watch. Anderson, he thought, and sat on the edge of his seat looking out. In a few minutes he'd change buses and be on the last short lap to Oclonee.

He hardly waited for the bus to stop before he got down his worn suitcase and hurried to the door bumping it along the sides of the aisle seats as he went.

Nothing wrong with me, he thought, walking straight through the neon lit station filled with holidaying people to the ramp on the other side where the Oclonee bus would load. He thumped his suitcase down and rested one foot on it, waiting. His depression had changed to a humming eagerness to get back to the house by the church.

Nothing wrong with me at all — except I probably kissed the wrong girl this Christmas.

It was not until after supper the next night that he got a chance to be alone with Eleanor. Cora had stuck maddeningly close, filled with questions and instant information.

"Annelle Wilkinson's pregnant," she'd announced at once. "First time in eight years. We're all hoping this will be the boy Johnny's been wanting. S. P. Willard got roaring drunk New Year's Day and painted a whole side of the Court House royal blue. Joe says he's had it with S. P."

Nathan tried to listen but worried instead about Eleanor who seemed to have retreated in his short absence into the awkward shyness she'd felt when he first moved in.

That girl needs a steady tending to, he thought.

He almost pushed Cora out the door to her class meeting after supper and hurried back to the kitchen where Eleanor had started the dishes. Leaning against the cupboard by the sink watching her he decided it was not shyness that troubled her — she seemed so distracted over some worry that she hardly knew he was present.

He got a towel off the the door and took a dish she had washed twice out of her hand to dry it.

"Rough day at the old education plant?" he asked.

90

"Oh so, so."

"Principal doesn't appreciate you? Kid steal your recess apple?"

"Oh, Nathan!" She smiled at last, but with the shadow of sadness drifting across the smile.

"What's really bothering you, my little friend?"

Eleanor didn't answer, just stared out the dark window behind the sink. Nathan stopped polishing the dish in his hand, prickles of alarm tightening his stomach. "Buddy?"

She nodded, her face averted. "I didn't know he was even in town. I ran into him yesterday on the street and purely panicked. I couldn't think of three words to put together sensibly." She shook her head, still looking out the window. "I had conned myself into thinking I was all over him, and then I saw him. All I had to do was just see him."

"He has to keep running back!"

She came immediately to Buddy's defense. "This is his home. You can't blame him for coming back!"

Nathan threw his dish towel on the sink. "You mean *you* can't blame him."

"Nathan . . ."

"I'm sorry, El'na. I know it's been rough, but it's also been three years now. You've got to get over this guy, I mean really over him." He carefully put the dish in the cupboard. "Best thing for you to do is fall for some other fellow."

She looked up at him, gray eyes wide. "Nathan! I never will, I know I never will! Even if I could, who is there? Durwood Thigpen? Old Dr. Davison?"

Nathan saw no hint of laughter on her face. He answered wryly, "The supply is limited, I'll agree."

He laid his hand gently on her shoulder and she looked at him smiling, but he saw her mind was already back on that other face.

He started upstairs to write Julia a letter. *Might as well,* he thought, *the signals in this camp are still strictly negative.*

13

NATHAN FOUND THE MONTHS of January and February
interminable ones — for himself and apparently for his church
members. They were the coldest months. The sun was a su-
preme faker, illuminating everything and warming nothing.
In its clear gold the shapes and colors of things were enunci-
ated sharply, the sky flat blue, the clouds chiseled from white
marble, pointed spokes along the top of an iron fence black
icicles stabbing the air, the ocean a slate shivering into
splinters on the crystalline sand.

Before the wind everything flew, leaves and small branches,
clots of newspaper, a child's hair ribbon. They flew and
scraped along the pavement until stopped by something big
enough to stand against the broom sweep of the wind.

Christmas memories no longer brought any glow and
Easter was too far away to create the slightest excitement.

Nathan was chagrined to find that in the barrenness of
these days Rena was able to stir up new interest in last summer's scandal. His prayer covenant with her had evidently
run its course.

He rushed home one day hoping to get a quick lunch so he
could get to Anderson for a Bible School planning clinic.
One look at Cora and he knew lunch would take time.

Her eyes were red and her face strained as if she had been
crying a long while. He made a try at pretending not to
notice but her silence held only until dessert.

"I just don't know what I'm going to do!" she burst out.

"About what?"

"About everything. But especially about these." She pulled
several pieces of paper from her apron pocket, unfolded
them and spread them before him.

They were anonymous notes. The first two said, "You're
not fit to belong to the church," and "You're as dirty as that

other woman." No wonder Corrie was so upset. He pulled the third one toward him. It read, "We know it was Eleanor."

Nathan slammed his hand down on the notes. "How could anybody suspect Eleanor!" He stood up, pushing back his chair. "She's not only too fine to have gotten into such a mess — they ought to know —! Don't they know how she feels about Buddy?"

Cora spoke softly. "Maybe that right there has something to do with it. They might reason she was feeling so low, she just latched on to Billy in a weak moment."

Nathan was aghast. "Cora! How can you even suggest..." he paused, remembering that Cora was in a position to do more than suggest. "Forget it," he said abruptly. "It was just a rhetorical question."

"What?"

"Nothing."

"Myrtle came right after I got them. She thinks I should have told all I knew at the start. She says it's gotten so that now everybody is under suspicion ... that the older women stand around looking at the young ones, smirking, and trying to guess which one it is. She says her Dolly has gotten downright sensitive, me and Myrtle being best friends."

"Oh, good night, Cora," he said, looking worriedly at his watch. "I'm trying to put my mind on progress in this church. I am trying to get other people's minds on progress. There are things that need doing, immediately. This scandal has gotten all out of proportion — it's standing in the way of what I'm trying to do."

"Is that my fault?"

"Of course not, Corrie," he said more kindly. "I know you have acted from high motives, but like Myrtle, I wish sometimes you had spilled the whole thing when it first happened or that Bill had, or this plagued girl, whoever she is, had given herself away." He turned to go. Unless it was Eleanor. Ridiculous. It absolutely could not be Eleanor.

"And these notes?" Cora said.

"Burn 'em. You know that Rena either wrote them or put someone else up to writing them. I am going to fix her. I am just going to have to fix her."

"That'll be the day," Cora said.

By the time Nathan returned to Oclonee that night he had thought of a dozen ways to get at Rena, and discarded most of them. With so many of the adult women corraled in her Sunday school class, the husbands of these women holding key positions, and her own husband Chairman of the Board of Deacons, Rena simply wasn't an easy stump to move.

He was determined to move her. For the sake of the church. For his own sake. And the only way he could see to get started was to make some kind of inroad on her class.

When he drove past the Petrie house it was dark. He looked up its angular height to the cupola at the top of a turret.

"Just you wait, my sister," he whispered through his teeth, and when well past the house he added, "you beak-nosed biddy."

A few days later Nathan waited uneasily in his study for a call from Alice Stevens.

Determined to start whittling on Rena's powers he had sent Alice and Dolly to see her, to tell her specifically that they intended to slice off with others into a young matron's class, that the new class would indeed begin informally this very week in Alice's home. They wanted her to know it because they didn't want her to think they were acting behind her back.

Nathan didn't offer to go along. Alice snatched at his idea, eager for aggressive action. Dolly hung back, obviously frightened, until coerced by Alice with some feminine logic Nathan didn't understand but for which he was grateful.

Now he waited for Alice's call and worried, drumming his fingers on his desk. He hoped neither of them had a mortgage at the bank.

At last the phone rang and he snatched at the receiver.
"Preacher?"
"Alice! What happened?"
"Nothing, absolutely nothing."
"What?"

"That's right. She didn't say yea and she didn't say nay. She just looked her usual righteous self and thanked us for coming.
"Hmmmm."

"What do you think, preacher?"

"I don't know what to think. I guess we'll have to wait and see what happens, that's all. In the meantime, go on with your meeting."

Nathan waited nervously for three days. On Sunday night after the evening service he came into his study and found three men sitting in a stiff row on his couch. He had the immediate impression that his waiting was over.

Standing behind his desk he looked into the solemn faces of Henry Buchanan, Carlisle Beck and Ashley Poole. Nathan had these three men pretty well pegged, though he didn't really know what to expect of Carlisle. He was usually a quiet man and a serious one, almost dour, but genial enough on the regular visits Nathan made to his barber's chair. Tonight he seemed more dour than genial.

The hair on the back of his neck prickling a warning, Nathan sat down, folded his hands on the desk blotter and forced a pleasant smile.

"Well, gentlemen, did you want to talk to me about something?"

Henry cleared his throat. "The deacons had a special meeting this afternoon to talk about the Sunday school."

Nathan raised his eyebrows. He had not known about the meeting — but he really couldn't make an issue of it since he himself had bypassed Henry in starting the new class.

"We talked about our whole set-up and we three have been asked to come here and tell you to stop this foolishness about cutting up Rena's class."

A spark of anger flared in Nathan's stomach. He frowned slightly at Henry. "Foolishness?" he asked.

"Yes, the deacons think so. You're upsetting people, that's what you're doing. Why, you will tear up the church if you're not careful."

The spark caught fire and burned, but Nathan said calmly, "Will I now?"

"And another thing," Ashley Poole broke in. "The deacons think that as the preacher you ought to be able to do something about this everlasting Thompson scandal."

"And what would the deacons suggest that I do?"

"It ain't our job to tell you how to do your job," Ashley said, his head stretching taller out of his loose collar.

"Now, uh, Brother Waite," Carlisle said, "we thought that since you live at Cora's maybe you could use your influence to get her to, uh . . ."

"Rat?" Nathan snapped.

Ashley glared, his Adam's apple jerking.

"Well, Brother Waite, that's rather distasteful language," Carlisle said.

"I'm sorry."

"Yes, of course, well, you see there's another problem. It's even more delicate."

Ashley interrupted. "But it ought to be dealt with openly. The plain truth is, Preacher, that some people think Eleanor Boyette's the guilty one, and that kind of puts you in a bad light, living there, and all."

Nathan rose, braced on rigid fingers and with lowered head fixed his eyes on Ashley. "And all what, Mr. Poole?"

Ashley put up his hands and waved Nathan down. "I didn't go to accuse you of anything, Preacher. I for one think that whatever mistakes you've made is because you lack experience. I'm just trying to tell you for your own good what some people are saying and others are probably thinking."

Nathan was so filled with fury that he dared not form a syllable. He stood there staring at them, fighting back the anger scalding his throat.

The three men rose as one.

"There's no need for you to get so wrought up," Ashley said. "The deacons are just trying to do their duty by you and the church. All we ask is for you to think on what we've said."

Holding their hats in their hands they eased out of his study. When they had gone Nathan sprinted to the door and sent it crashing shut.

She did it! I know she did it! He whirled around, raging. *Blast her scroungy hide!*

He leaned his arm against a book shelf and rolled his head back and forth in helpless fury. He had not budged her. She had slammed his puny effort back in his face. But she had to have a vulnerable side and when he found out which one it was—

Nathan slept little that night. He turned from one position to another, but in no position did his anger or his frustration abate. In a half sleeping state each part of his bed became symbolic of a portion of his nightmare, so that turning, he did not rest, only relived a grinding emotion. The last clock chime he counted numbered three.

It seemed not more than fifteen minutes later he thought he heard it chime again. He opened his eyes to blink at a frosted window pane, glittering in the sun.

The telephone rang again.

He stumbled across the floor, his feet freezing on the bare boards, pulled on his robe and groped his way down the steps to the hall phone.

It was Dr. Davison. While Nathan had tossed in miserable sleeplessness, influenza had claimed one of his church members for Death.

14

THE TELEPHONE IN Nathan's study rang repeatedly that morning as news of Aunt Sally Lennon's death moved across town. Shocked church members called to be sure he knew about it for it seemed no one had known she was even sick until a neighbor had heard the cats crying at the kitchen door and gone to see what was the matter.

"Too busy gossipin' to know," Cora said.

And then the telephone rang again, and it wasn't about Aunt Sally. There had been another death in the early hours of the morning. Nathan cradled the telephone slowly and stared for a moment in the silence of shock. Sarah Sue Warren, seven months pregnant, was dead of the flu in Anderson.

Nathan drove immediately to the school to tell Eleanor and take her home. She insisted instead that he take her to Miss Alma's.

"I'm the closest family she's got until Buddy comes."

Nathan worried because she held back her tears. "Don't try to be so brave," he said.

"I'm not brave. I'm numb. The only thing I can think of is that I should have tried harder for a genuine reconciliation. I have been so filled with my own hurt I never thought how hard it was for her to live away from her own home and old friends, like a criminal, like an exile."

"You made a start at Christmas, El'na. You made a real start. Now be grateful for that and don't punish yourself."

"I am grateful," she said. "I am grateful."

He followed her worriedly as she went dry-eyed into the house to find Miss Alma.

Nathan, tense over the thought of having to conduct two funerals the same day, was relieved when a nephew of Aunt Sally's told him the family wanted to ask Brother LeRoy to come back for her service. One of Aunt Sally's friends had reminded them of her long years of service with Brother LeRoy and her own stated wish that he come back to put her away.

Nathan thought it would be perfectly all right and told the family so. He couldn't accuse Brother LeRoy of keeping a path worn back to his old field, as some preachers did. As far as Nathan knew the old gentleman had not been back since he himself had arrived in Oclonee. It seemed a little poetic to Nathan that the old man would bury this old lady with whom he'd served so many years.

Going from Aunt Sally's to Miss Alma's he discovered that Miss Alma had heard that Brother LeRoy was coming and wanted to have him conduct Sarah Sue's funeral service too. This didn't seem at all poetic, particularly when Gertrude Beck quoted Miss Alma's reasoning. "After all," she'd wailed, "the new little preacher didn't really know our Sarah Sue."

There was nothing that he could do except assure Buddy that it was fine, and that he would be glad to offer prayer at Sarah Sue's funeral as he would at Aunt Sally's.

"We appreciate your being so understanding," Buddy said. "Mrs. Petrie told us that you would."

"Mrs. Petrie?"

"She was kind enough to help Mama and me decide what we wanted to do."

"She is very good at things like that," Nathan said, and Buddy nodded, accepting his statement at surface value.

Nathan knew that was the way he had to play it — the right words — the right gestures. After all, these people were stricken in their grief, it was not in them to act spitefully, nor should he punish them for what he was sure was spitefulness in other quarters.

Rena's motives were obvious. Brother LeRoy's? He would reserve his opinion of dear old Brother LeRoy.

The old gentleman came the morning before the funerals and Nathan met him in his study. Brother LeRoy looked harmless enough. He was tall in spite of stooped shoulders. The lines of his handsome face were hazed over by time, the top of his head smooth as old ivory, the sides of his face fringed with hair as fine as a dandelion gone to seed.

He took Nathan's hand in the softness of his old one. "While we have these quiet minutes together, I want to thank you for allowing me to come back for these services. I appreciate it deeply. I baptized little Sarah Sue, and Sally Lennon, God bless her, she was dear to me, dear to me."

Nathan removed his hand, afraid the old man was going to cry. "I'm glad you could come," he said. "Sit down, won't you?"

"Thank you, sir." He looked around the room and then over at Nathan's desk and chair. "Now you won't be offended with me if I sit down there for a few minutes for old times sake?"

"Of course not," Nathan said, trying to avoid expressing the stiffness he felt.

Brother LeRoy sat down and leaned back comfortably, at ease in a well known spot. "I'm so glad to meet my successor," he said. "I hear good things about you."

Oh, spare me that, Nathan thought. "Come now, Rev. LeRoy, I'm sure you've heard more bad than good."

"Oh, of course, I know you've drawn fire from certain stations. That doesn't surprise me. I had my snipers too, y'know."

"You? Why these people rate you somewhere among the Apostles."

Brother LeRoy laughed. "That's because I'm off the scene, and old. It helps to be old." He rocked gently in the swivel chair and then leaned forward, shifting Nathan's matched desk appointments about, running his fingers across the scratched and pocked surface of the old desk. "Ah," he said, "such memories."

Nathan got the picture of this quiet man, studying at this desk, praying at it, dispensing sweetness to people from it.

Brother LeRoy dipped his fingers into the deepest scar, the circular one, an eighth of an inch deep at one side, and Nathan felt apologetic. "I've meant to get some wood putty and fill that in," he said.

"Oh, I'd hate for you to do that. It would make me very sad for you to do that."

Nathan looked at him questioningly.

Brother LeRoy smiled. "It has to do with one of the times

I was under fire — the actual reasons don't matter for my tale. I was in here putting up drapery rods when a certain person called me on the telephone and proceeded to dress me down in no uncertain terms. I stood here, the phone in one hand, the hammer in the other — blazing like a pine tree in a forest fire. The farther she went the hotter I blazed and when she hung up on my attempt to defend my position — that did it! I dropped the receiver and swung that hammer at the desk with all the weight of my fury. Kapow!!! The shock hurt clean up in my shoulder — but it hurt grand!

"Afterwards, of course, I was ashamed, and fearful too. The desk was almost new at the time. I was always afraid someone would ask about that dent and I couldn't think of a way in the world to adequately explain it."

"No one asked?"

"No one asked. I kept my Bible on top of it. Not many church members would think of moving their preacher's Bible."

Nathan laughed. The old man fingered the scar again and Nathan, suspecting a moral was about to be delivered obligingly cued in his guest.

"I suppose that was a lesson of sorts and you never lost your patience with a church member and hit the desk again."

"Well, let's say I never hit the desk again. Right after that I took up golf."

He sat there enjoying his joke, smiling at Nathan and jerking his head a little at him, wanting him to enjoy it too. Nathan let him have the moment, but something else was nagging at his mind.

"Now then," he said, "you've confessed how you dented the desk, you'll have to tell me who riled you so fiercely."

Brother LeRoy put his fingers together and leaned back in the chair, smiling over Nathan's head, savoring old memories.

"It was Sally Lennon," he said.

After the funerals Nathan and Cora sat in the kitchen drinking coffee and eating some of the food friends had brought in. Eleanor had fled upstairs to her room as soon as they'd come home. *101*

"Can't you go to her?" Nathan burst out suddenly.

"No," Cora said. "Sometimes a woman has to cry alone."

Nathan, anxious, and impatient with his own anxiety, pushed back his chair and walked over to the kitchen window to stare out into the yard. The bare branches of the pecan tree looked like a pencil sketch against a pink and gray sunset.

"I wish I could feel as calm and wise as you sound, Corrie. I tell you what else is bugging me. I've got to go see Worth tomorrow."

Cora clucked her tongue against the roof of her mouth. "Annie says she's afraid he'll get this flu. Weak as he is he can't stand the flu. He'd be the third one. Death comes in threes, y'know."

"Don't say that. That's superstition, not wisdom."

Nathan went unwillingly to see Worth. He'd tried to go once since his first barren call, but Annie herself had stopped him at the door.

"It's one of his bad days," she said. "You'd best come back when he's more peaceable."

"You mean there are days when he is peaceable?"

She smiled and patted his arm. "More peaceable, I said."

Now she'd asked him to come, stating plainly that Worth was in no way easier to approach, but that she was afraid for him. She didn't know how long any of them had to get this boy right with God.

At the Parker house he shivered in the wind sweeping off the river and straight across the wide porch. Both Annie and Mr. Parker were out and the cook let him in. She took his hat and coat, walked him to Worth's door and left him on his own.

Nathan tapped lightly, afraid Worth might be asleep and hoping he was sound asleep and wouldn't hear the door.

"Come in if you must."

Nathan entered. The room was too hot. A fire well piled with wood burned briskly in the grate. Worth's face was red and he looked distraught.

"How are you, Worth?"

102   "I'm like I was yesterday and will be tomorrow."

"Well, at least you're not worse," Nathan tried to laugh easily.

"Very humorous."

Nathan shifted on his feet, uncertain whether he should sit down.

"Ah, does it seem warm in here to you?" he asked and then worried because maybe Worth had to have it this warm.

"Of course, it's too warm. And that worthless Annie better get herself back here."

Nathan started to ask if there was something he could do. Instead he went to the window and lowered it very slightly from the top. Then he caught the edge of a counterpane over Worth's body, assured himself there was a blanket underneath, and pulled it back, folding it well off of Worth's feet.

"When you want that back, whistle," he said and sat down.

Worth turned his head and looked out the window.

A row of frozen poinsettias trembled against the fence and the evergreens near the house were dully dark. A sparrow flew to the window sill, puffed out his feathers and looked in at the men.

"Looks like he might be waiting for a free lunch."

"Annie feeds them."

"Do you see many varieties?"

"I'm no bird watcher!"

They were silent. The sparrow despaired and flew away. Nathan fretted. How to take hold?

"Did Annie send you?" Worth asked, face still averted.

"Well, she asked me to come."

Worth laughed without humor and turned to Nathan. "She's afraid for my eternal soul. I try to tell her, I have no eternal soul, so she doesn't have to be afraid."

When Nathan didn't answer immediately he laughed again. "Aren't you going to seize this chance to work on a real live atheist?"

Nathan said slowly, "Suppose I told you I don't believe there is such a thing as an atheist?"

"Then I would say you're a fool or else you're younger than you look."

Nathan bridled. "I know a minister who has served far longer than I. He says a man is an atheist until he gets into bad trouble."

Worth did not answer. He smiled a half smile and stared deep into Nathan's eyes.

Nathan could not turn from the gaze. He felt a wave, first of embarrassment and then of pain sweep over him. He burst out, "My God, that was a stupid thing to say to you! I'm sorry."

Worth's smile was bitter. "It's the typical sort of thing people say to me. That's why I don't want anyone coming here."

"Worth — I had hoped we might be friends."

Worth laughed. "Ha! The preacher and the atheist. Now that's a provocative pair." He paused a moment, "But of course, I'm not always an atheist." His face grave, his eyes mocked Nathan.

"No, I vary from day to day. Some days I am calm. These are the days I am an atheist. Some days I believe in God, and these are the days I rage and curse Him for what He has done to me!"

Nathan felt cold in the hot room. "Don't talk that way," he said.

"I frighten you, don't I? I frighten you and Annie because you think God will strike me dead and throw me into hell."

"That's not quite my theology," Nathan said stiffly.

"Why don't you go home, Waite?"

"I wish there was some way I could reach you."

"There isn't. Give up. Go away and talk to people who want to listen."

Nathan rose slowly and looked around uncertainly. He was trembling, but the fire still roared in its grate. "Shall I close the window?"

"No! I'll not burn now and later too."

"I'll come back."

"Don't come back. I don't want your friendship, or your religion."

Just as Nathan got to the door Worth called to him. "By the way, preacher," the motionless man said, "if I ever came to God it wouldn't be from fear. What kind of a God would that be, to draw a man in fear?"

104 Nathan opened his mouth to speak, but Worth said, "Good-by, preacher."

Nathan got his coat and let himself out the door.

15

ON A WINDY AFTERNOON, warm in the sun, cool in the shade, Nathan sat in the kitchen morosely nursing a cup of coffee, in no hurry to get on with "the work." He had in fact felt no enthusiasm for his work in Oclonee for what seemed now like several painfully drawn-out eons. A letter from Julia this morning which ordinarily would have given him a lift was having an opposite effect.

He had fed Julia a line about his church and himself as its leader. If she knew what kind of a situation he was really hung up in she'd mark him off her list for good. He had to have some kind of success story to make the grade with that chick and he knew it. Especially with her dear brother going great guns in Atlanta.

He flinched as the front door opened and slammed in the wind. Eleanor came into the kitchen grinning, her cheeks red from the cold, a spray of pear blossoms in her hand. Waving it for him to see she announced, "Spring!"

"Not yet," he said, scowling at the flowers.

"It's coming"

"Maybe."

She grinned, undaunted, and Nathan felt better in spite of himself. "Hey, Mary Poppins," he said, "let's go to the beach. I need to walk off some of my bile."

When she raised her eyebrows he said, "Don't tell me we can't. We'll take Cora. She can sit in the car and crochet while we walk."

Cora was quite agreeable and he took the further precaution of putting Eleanor in the back seat of the car, and Cora in the front where she smiled broadly at everyone they passed.

They came alongside of Laura Adams walking along the sidewalk toward the Post Office with a handful of mail and Cora waved happily to her and then sighed in deep satisfaction.

"Durwood took Laura to the picture show again last night. That makes three times that I know of," she said.

"Then there must not be but three times," Nathan teased.

"What? Oh you hush." She giggled. "I'm bettin' Durwood's looking for a safe harbor from a certain storm, not mentioning any names."

Nathan glanced over his shoulder at Eleanor. "You been chasin' Durwood again, El'na?"

"Oh, I'd hoped you wouldn't notice."

"Foot," Cora said. "El'na ain't studyin' Durwood. You know who I mean."

"I know who you mean, lady, and I don't care, as long as she isn't chasing me."

He looked in the rear view mirror to see if Eleanor was appreciating him. She was.

At the beach Nathan drove along the paved street paralleling the dunes until he was well past the string of rental houses and permanent homes, and then turned in to park on a shell paved side road that cut through the dunes to the beach and the surf.

Leaving Cora in the car they started walking down the hard packed sand, the wind in their faces, cold but not bitter, the sun bright on the sand, the gray-green ocean rolling peacefully and with no threats to anything larger than the periwinkle shells swirling in the lacy foam near their feet.

They did not talk. They walked with their hands shoved deep in their pockets, and when they had gotten as far along the beach as Nathan supposed Cora could clearly see them he said, "We'd better go back toward our duenna."

Eleanor giggled but Nathan could not smile. "It's ridiculous," he said to her laughing mouth.

"I agree," she said, still smiling.

Nathan sighed. When they were almost in front of where the car was parked he said, "Let's go up where the sand is dry and sit down for a few minutes." Sitting in the sand he drew up his knees and leaned his arms on them, staring out at the ocean.

Eleanor tied a scarf around her head. Looking at him from under her lashes she asked, "What's the matter, Nathan?"

He rested his chin on his arms. "Nothing that a change in churches wouldn't cure."

"Nathan, it's not that bad."

He raised his head. "Isn't it? My dear Miss Boyette, I foolishly spent part of this morning reviewing my ministry in this church. I can truthfully say that I can point to no successful project completed or even launched, no rehabilitated member, and no new members other than a couple of kids who would have joined if Donald Duck had been the preacher. Not only have I not accomplished anything, I am up against an impasse. I admit I may have helped build it in my youthful exuberance, but it's there and I see no hope of budging it."

She smoothed and patted the sand at her feet. "I know some of the things that have happened are discouraging to you — even depressing."

"Are you kidding? I don't feel good enough to be depressed."

She drew small swirls in the soft sand. "I guess it's different for you, but I've grown up in this church. I'm used to the people. I've seen them at their worst and at their best, and over the long sweep it sort of evens out."

Nathan scowled. "Well, I am not used to them and I simply don't have time to wait to get the big picture. I'm a young man. I've got things to do, places to go."

"And you will go, and you will do these things. I know that, Nathan. But you're here now, and what you do here, will surely affect you there."

Nathan smiled wryly into the troubled gray eyes looking into his.

"Now that's a tidy bit of philosophy for this early in the day."

She ducked her head. "I don't mean to preach."

"That's right. You leave the preaching to the Right Reverend Mr. Waite."

When she looked at him again her face was quite serious. With a tentative note in her voice she said, "Corrie tells me

Miss Alma's asked you to deliver the lecture at the DAR dedication this summer."

Nathan jerked his head impatiently. "And did she tell you I told Miss Alma I didn't think I could do it?"

She nodded. "Why not?"

"Because I know that behind Miss Alma's gracious invitation stands a string pulling Rena Petrie. Eleanor, she thinks she's got me bested and that now all she has to do is twinge a lever and away I'll dance. Except that's the wrong metaphor. Rena doesn't approve of dancing."

"I don't think that's it at all, Nathan."

"Don't you?"

"I think that this may be Rena's way of holding out an olive branch. DAR is very big in her life, and dedicating this marker is the biggest DAR function I can remember in Oclonee. People are coming from the state Historical Society and even one representative from Washington. So if Rena nudged Miss Alma into inviting you to give the main address it has to mean she wants to make up."

"Hah! Rena can take the entire DAR and go you know where."

Eleanor sighed. "Nathan, look, there's a great deal involved here. This dedication may seem a bunch of nothing to you, but to a lot of the older people in your church and in this community it's a significant event. If you make light of it you make light of their feelings. I think you have to care about people's feelings."

He looked at her with suspicion. "Are you preaching again?"

She shook her head affirmatively. "Yes, I am. I think you ought to not only accept the invitation, you ought to give a lecture on American history and responsibility that will add all kinds of depth and dimension to the occasion."

She emphasized her words with a broad sweep of her hand, her face earnest and confident he could do just that. Nathan felt the tightness that had constricted his chest for weeks miraculously dissolve.

He caught her hand, laced his fingers with hers and lowered her hand to the soft sand between them.

"Yes, Miss Boyette," he said with gentle sarcasm, feeling

no resentment. He was amazed at his own feelings. It seemed completely right that she should counsel and encourage him. Just as it was right that she sit silent now, close beside him.

Eleanor smiled, not at him, playing in the sand with the fingers of her free hand, the ends of her bright hair curling around her scarf, her mouth soft in its smile.

I've got to kiss that mouth, he thought, and then checked himself, cursing his own stupidity. Cora sat behind them — at his own invitation. But he had not known an hour ago that he would feel this way, that he would need so desperately to begin to put words to his feelings, to demonstrate his feelings where there were no words.

Eleanor sat oblivious to his turmoil, gazing out to sea, pensive now but not sad. A new agony seized Nathan.

She'd better not be thinking of that blasted Buddy!

He tightened his grip on her hand, and as he did she moved her hand in his. "We'd better go," she said, "I've got some work I need to do."

He sprang up and pulled her to her feet. "Me too. I've got a lot of work I need to do."

And the best part of it was, he really thought he could do it.

16

Carlisle Beck stood at his barber's chair methodically trimming the preacher's sideburns. He was well aware that his work never pleased Nathan completely, but then Nathan's work never pleased him completely either. He saw Nathan steal a nervous glance in the mirror as a little too much hair fell away.

With such a customer Carlisle couldn't really relax, not even on such a pleasant day when the open door of the shop let in the warm salt air to mix with the deep scent of soap lather and the sharp sweetness of April Showers hair tonic. It was the kind of day most men who came to the shop stretched their legs and went sort of limp in the chairs, not getting excited even when they talked politics.

The preacher tensed a little more when Carlisle moved with the clippers to the back of his neck and then as if to show he wasn't really worried threw out a question.

"How about old Durwood and Laura?"

Kenny, who didn't have a customer and didn't care about that at all, spun his empty chair and laughed. "That's one for the books, huh? Everybody thought Alberta was bound to trip him up sooner or later and Laura beat her to it."

The preacher said, "Laura's quiet. It's those quiet ones you have to watch."

Carlisle frowned at Kenny just as he was about to give his chair another spin. Kenny shrugged and leaned on it instead. "The women are having fits," he said to Nathan. "Between this wedding and the DAR dedication they're just about to be translated."

Carlisle reluctantly put away his shears. He would really have liked to take off more of the preacher's hair. He loosened the towel instead and began dusting inside the preacher's collar with a soft, full brush.

"Phew, Brother Beck," Nathan said, "you'll have me smelling like a rose bush."

"Hah. The better to please the ladies," Kenny said. "Say, Preacher, when you going to get hitched anyway, so all us married men can quit worrying about our wives?"

Carlisle frowned, really put out with Kenny.

The preacher said, "The Bible says a man with a wife thinks of his wife when he ought to be thinking of his work."

Kenny laughed, "Yeah, but it also says, it's better to marry than to..." He stopped abruptly as a lady entered with a small boy.

"How do, Miz Peirce," Carlisle said. They all waited while she settled the boy in a chair and left.

"Seriously, now," Nathan said, "I don't know what I'd do if I had a family to keep up with. I have a non-stop schedule next week. I'm speaking at the banquet the Rotary Club is giving the high school seniors, and helping the Stevens chaperone the beach party the Kiwanians are sponsoring for them."

Kenny said, "You better watch yourself, Preacher, Alice Stevens ain't half bad in a bathing suit."

"That'll do!" Carlisle half shouted, slapping the back of his chair so hard the little boy in the next one jumped. Then Carlisle was embarrassed — at Kenny's behavior and his own. He took the preacher's money without looking at him. If the preacher were more serious minded maybe Kenny wouldn't say things like that to him.

He was relieved to see Johnny Wilkinson walk in.

"Well, hello there, papa!" Kenny said. "Congratulations, and how's the mama and baby?"

"Fine," Johnny said, folding himself into the chair where Nathan had been sitting.

"I heard about the baby," the preacher said. "Certainly am glad it's here. It was a boy, right?"

Johnny looked at the two barbers and smiled broadly. "Right," he said.

"This isn't just a boy, this is the boy, eh Johnny?" Kenny said.

The preacher got his coat off the rack. "Well, I want to get out and see Annelle one of these days when she gets to feeling like company. Thanks, Brother Beck. See you fellows at church." He paused. "Sure would be nice to see you there, Johnny."

"Sure. One of these days." He winked at Kenny. "Might let you baptize the boy for me."

Carlisle frowned. "Johnny's ribbing you, Brother Waite," he explained. "He knows better."

The preacher smiled and waved at the men and the little boy. "See you," he said again and left.

Carlisle cranked Johnny's chair down a notch. "You ought not to tease the preacher," he said.

"Ah, he don't care," Kenny said. "He don't care if you tease him."

Johnny stretched his long legs out to hang over the foot rest. "That preacher don't care about nothing," he said, "except maybe about himself."

Nathan walked briskly away from the barber shop, trying to outdistance his sense of unease. Clearly, he had muffed that whole bit.

Involved in his own feeling he almost passed Buddy Warren standing by a pick up truck in front of a vacant lot. He had seen Buddy several times since Sarah Sue's death in January. Buddy had seemed eager to form a friendly alliance and now hailed him enthusiastically. Nathan responded with more politeness than pleasure.

"What brings you to the big city of Oclonee?" Nathan asked.

"It doesn't take much of an excuse to bring me here," Buddy said, "however I am here today on serious business. I'm not broadcasting the news yet, but I don't mind your knowing. I'm coming back to Oclonee in a few months, to live. "I've got a franchise to sell Fords.

He pointed to the vacant lot and then pulled his fingers across his lower lip as if thinking hard. "I've got to build a shop and I'm considering this lot. What do you think?"

Nathan raised his eyebrows and pursed his lips. "Oh, it's a good location," he said, thinking of another he'd prefer.

Buddy positively grinned. "I'm really looking forward to moving back home. I want to get settled, for Little Buddy's sake as well as my own. I'm anxious to get active in this community again."

Nathan nodded his head. *I'll just bet you are.*

"Well," he said, "good luck to you, with your shop. Be seeing you around."

He walked away from Buddy down the sidewalk, whistling fiercely through his teeth.

When he came into the house by the church an hour later an unexpected sound met his ears. Eleanor was singing.

He stopped, hands still on the coat he had been hanging up. Why was the little gray swallow suddenly a mocking bird? In a moment his suspicion was confirmed. In the kitchen Cora paused in her pot banging to call, "Is that you, Nathan?"

"Yes."

"Did you hear about Buddy?"

"I heard, I heard," he said, stomping up the stairs.

At Supper Cora said, "Did you get by to see the Wilkinson baby today?"

"No, I didn't," he said crossly. "Why does everyone make such a big deal out of that one little baby?"

"Well, it is kind of a special baby y' know, Johnny wanting him so long, and Myrtle said she heard it actually ain't real well. I know it would mean a lot to all of them if you'd go see it."

He sighed. "I know I should go, and I will, but you ought to see the list of visits I need to make on my own members."

"Well, Johnny and Annelle ought to be our members. Maybe if you ..."

"Look, my omnipresent conscience, I said I'd go see the baby. Believe me, I'll go."

Cora had the last word. "Try to make it before he starts kindergarten," she said.

17

Two weeks later Nathan still hadn't seen the Wilkinson baby. Glancing at his watch he saw he wouldn't have time to go today either. Buck and Alice would be picking him up for the Senior picnic within minutes. Pressed as he was for time Nathan stayed at his desk long enough to organize it neatly before heading home.

He had just changed clothes and collected his bathing suit and towel when Buck honked. Running through the hall he nearly collided with Eleanor. "You did get home in time," he said. "That's great!" Shifting his roll of clothes he tried to take the ever present load of books from her arms. "Now come on and go to the beach with us. The kids would love it."

She laughed and tried to retrieve her possessions. "I can't, Nathan, I told you this morning," and as he held on to the books, "Nathan, you're keeping the Stevens waiting."

"You're keeping the preacher waiting, my girl. Get your suit. I'll teach you to fish."

This time she pulled at her books with such firmness he knew she meant it. "That's one thing you can't teach me," she said unsmilingly, "I know how to fish."

He let her go but when she was at her door called out, "Party pooper!"

She turned around and relaxed her face in a grin. "I don't mean to be."

He blew her a kiss. "I know it, hon." Buck blew the horn again. "Don't work too hard," Nathan said and ran down the stairs.

Apologizing for the delay he climbed in the front seat by Alice. She was wearing pink Bermuda shorts with a matching monogrammed shirt and white sandals on her brown feet.

"You look good as usual, Miss Alice," he said.

Buck hit the starter abruptly and when they were underway asked, "Why didn't you bring Eleanor?"

"I was trying to, that's why I was late. She said she had to study."

"There was a time she wouldn't have turned down a fishing trip," Buck said.

"Oh?"

"She and Buddy used to be ring leaders in this kind of party."

Nathan dropped his head and pretended to tie a shoe lace.

Alice said, "Oh well, if you'd brought her it probably would just have caused a lot of gossip. You know the women of Oclonee." She spoke with some rancor.

Nathan finished tying his shoe laces and looked out the window. He knew the women of Oclonee.

Buck leaned around Alice a moment to speak to Nathan. "Not to change the subject, but how'd the deacon's meeting go last night? Anything new?"

"Oh, nothing spectacular. The main thing we talked about was the prospect of a revival. You know I've stalled it before, and I tried again last night, but it seems, 'We've always had a late summer revival.' "

"That's right," Buck said. "Why? Are you against it?"

"I'm against bringing guest speakers of any kind here with the church in the crummy condition it's in. It's humiliating to me personally even if it doesn't bother the brethren."

"Yeah, well, it gave you a good arguing point anyway."

"Oh, I didn't argue very strongly. I couldn't really argue against a revival could I? In a Baptist church?"

Buck gripped the steering wheel and hunched over it, frowning.

"Well, could I?"

Buck's face had gotten fiery red. "I don't know. *You're* the preacher, and *you* didn't want a revival this year. And it sure seems to me you had a leverage point on the painting question. You should have said, 'Either we paint or we don't have the revival!' "

"Hey, Buck, your blood pressure's showing," Alice said.

"I don't care. If Nathan doesn't get some ground rules

established pretty soon he's going to lose the whole ball game."

Nathan said nothing. He sat looking out the window of the car, a little angry with Buck and wondering if he ought to be angry with himself. He had given up pretty easily, but really, it would have been wrong to fight having a revival for a surface reason like the physical condition of the church. *Who am I kidding?* he thought. *I didn't want a row with the deacons, that's all, not right now.*

He looked across Alice to Buck's still pouting face. *He's really disappointed in me,* he thought. He turned back to stare out the window where the flat marshes had turned into sand dunes covered by wind broken scrub oaks.

He wished he could just say easily: *Be patient with me, Buck. Give me time to net the old guard, then I'll get back to you.*

They had fished, cooked and eaten supper, and were piling driftwood on the fire for a singing session when one of the boys who had gone walking down the beach came running back to say he had spotted a turtle coming up from the water.

"Let's go," some of the kids cried, and they all began to take off down the beach like long-legged sand crabs.

Nathan rubbed his hands down his bare chest. "I'm going back to the car after my shirt. I never saw a sea turtle."

When he came back they'd all gone except Alice.

"Aren't you a turtle fan?" he asked.

"Ugh," she said, and then, "besides, somebody has to keep the home fires burning. You go ahead. You won't have any trouble finding them."

"Oh, I'll just wait here," he said, hating to leave her alone. He eased down on the silky, warm sand beside her. "Help you tend the fire."

Alice's freckled face and bare arms glowed in the firelight and her short red hair whipped back and forth in the wind catching the tint of the flames whichever way it blew. Nathan idly poked at the coals with a long stem of sea oats. That Buck had sure outmarried himself.

He looked up, hearing someone coming toward them through the sand. It was Buck. He stopped, out of breath,

116

his face red and furious. "I thought you were with me," he said to Alice, and to Nathan, "and I thought you were coming right along."

Nathan felt embarrassed and accused. He struggled to his feet, not sure what one did with a church member who was also a jealous husband. He brushed off his hands on the seat of his pants. "Where'd they go? Will you show me?"

Buck was bent over wrenching at an unwieldy stump in the fire. "It's too late. They'll be back in a minute."

Nathan looked toward Alice. She had her knees drawn up, her arms folded across them and her head down on her arms. He wondered if she were very upset. When Buck kept his back to them, tending the fire, she rolled her head to look up at Nathan.

She was clearly not upset. If anything she was amused.

Har de har, he thought, very funny.

On the day of the wedding Nathan waited nervously in the hall back of the sanctuary door for his time to go in. The organ pealed out wedding music and in a moment the high ringing voice of Alberta Peeples began to tell the congregation that Durwood loved Laura truly or vice versa or both. She was in top form.

Amazed at the strength of her voice Nathan wondered how much of a disappointment this wedding really was for her. Her chase of Durwood had been as much a part of church lore as Laura's state of spinsterhood. If Alberta grieved she didn't show it. She went from the first splendid solo to the second without a waver.

When Nathan came in to take his place he saw the church was nearly full. Even Carlisle Beck had left the barber shop to come, looking somewhat unnerved by his holiday. Eleanor was sitting with Alma Warren instead of in her usual place by Cora and that unnerved Nathan.

Alice was there in a sharp new outfit, with Buck who seemed preoccupied with something unpleasant. Looking quickly past them Nathan saw that the Lesters and William Thompson had not come. Effie was there and Bill was too, sitting on opposite sides of the church. Rena, who had been conducted by an innocent young usher to the same pew with

Bill looked as taut as if she were wound tight and set to go off in an alarm at any moment.

Nathan tried to relax and see this service as the "truly happy occasion" Cora had predicted it would be. He couldn't. Not when he could feel the vibrations of a dozen criss-crossed wires humming just below the surface of the wedding finery.

When the organ's triumphant tones brought Laura down the aisle Cora took herself at her own word. She and Myrtle wept with joyful abandon into their best tatting edged handkerchiefs. Nathan envied them. They'd never raise an ulcer between them.

In his office afterward Nathan took time to read his mail. He was in no hurry to get to the wedding reception.

The congregation was. In a matter of minutes the church emptied and the sudden quiet was startling. Feeling like a child left out of a party he got up to go where the happiness was.

In the hall he stopped, hearing a small noise in the supply room. Some of the kids stealing chalk again? He tiptoed down the hall and opened the door which was slightly ajar. Inside, standing in the dark, a woman hunched over, her face in her hands.

Nathan tried to back up quietly, but as his hand left the doorknob it clicked loudly and she looked up. Her dismay at seeing him was brief and before she jerked her face away he saw a look of something like hatred cross it.

There was nothing for him to do but keep backing away and he did, knowing he should not have seen Alberta Peeples cry.

Nathan went to the reception with an uneasy mind, but needn't have worried. Alberta was not in the receiving line and the other guests were rather determinedly having a good time.

He was moving from group to group, working his way toward Eleanor, when he became aware that silence was spreading across the room. Billy Thompson had come in.

Now the atmosphere in the room swung rapidly from hush

to hilarity, back and forth, as the crowd tried to adjust itself to Bill's presence in this informal social gathering.

Ignoring them all Bill went straight to the refreshment table where Effie was helping and held up a plate to her to be served.

Effie picked up a silver cake knife with a snap of her wrist, and then paused, holding it over the cake with her face gone blank of expression. Then as suddenly as she'd picked it up she let it fall and turning sharply on her high heels ran out of the room. The two girls who had been standing near gave little cries and dashed after her.

Bill was left holding the plate. After a moment he eased it back down on the table, and turning, threw out his empty hands at his old friends.

In the nervous pause Effie's shrill voice carried to them from a bedroom, "The gall . . . the gall . . ." Bill shrugged wearily and went out through the kitchen. Nathan wasn't sure for whom he felt sorriest.

He waited until the conversation began again in fits and starts and then headed for the kitchen. Bill had stopped at the back steps and was sitting there in a huddle.

Nathan got two cups of coffee and went out to sit with him.

"Thanks, Preacher," Bill said, holding his cup in both hands and staring into the darkening yard. Then he shuddered. "I should have gone on off and joined the army. Vietnam couldn't be worse than this. I intended to go at first, but I thought she would forgive me and that if I hung around she'd forgive me sooner. I was wrong."

Inside the crowd laughed. Bill jerked his head toward the sound. "It's them knowing about it that makes it so bad. She can't give in with them knowing about it."

"Don't you think they would all forget it if you and Effie could get back together?"

"Oh, maybe after about a hundred years. I'm done in this town. No use hanging around agonizing over it."

Nathan shuffled his feet on the steps. "Give it a little more time, Bill. It can't get any worse. That is," he hesitated, "if you still love Effie."

Bill poured the last drops of his coffee, drop by drop on the grass by the steps. "I still love Effie. She knows it, that's why she does like she does. She's hurting me and she knows it. She's got to keep punishing me, I guess. I've tried to tell her that what happened was just a little flare-up thing that didn't matter. I've told her I'm sorry. God knows I'm sorry!"

Someone's shadow from the kitchen fell across them. Whoever made the shadow laughed nervously and went away. Bill handed Nathan his cup and stood up.

"I'll not go in again," he said. "I'm sorry I loused up the party." He stopped at the foot of the steps as if there might be another message and then went on through the dark yard.

Nathan reluctantly rejoined the newly boisterous guests in the living room. Looking around he saw that Eleanor had gone home. He wanted to go too. The party was lively, the room swinging with celebrators, but for him, nobody was there.

18

JOSEPHINA FINISHED making up her bed as ordered and went over to her window. She unlatched the screen and leaned out as far as she could go, turning her head from side to side and looking up and as far over the house as she could see.

"A beautiful day," she announced to the day itself. "It's not raining anywhere in the whole wide world."

Out in the hall she assured herself by listening over the bannister that her mama and daddy were busy talking before easing down the steps and out the front door. Slipping around the side of the house she crawled up under the kitchen window to check her buried treasure. She dug into the loose black sand until it turned damp and then she found her pieces of broken glass pushed tight, pressing summer flowers.

Inside the kitchen her mama said, "Joe, I'll leave your lunch in the refrigerator. Me and Corrie are going to hear the preacher speak at the DAR Dedication."

"That's fine with me long as you don't ask me to go," her daddy said, and then, "Where's S. P.? He hasn't been around for a couple of days."

"Oh, he's working. Doing some painting at the school while it's closed."

"Hmph. Works and then drinks up his pay. Well, he better not let me catch him drunk again and making a fool of himself. I'm going to call the police myself next time and tell them to put him under the jail."

"Oh, Joe . . ."

"I mean it. I don't want him staggering around here with his ugly drunk talk anymore. Josephina's got so old now we can't hide the truth much longer."

Josephina began edging away from the house on her hands and knees. She slipped through the shrubbery to the back end of the yard and then out through the broken place in the fence. Leaning back against the comforting rough warmth of the wide boards she took deep breaths, her stomach heaving.

"I gotta go warn him," she whispered. Her hands and head flat against the fence she eased along the wooden slats until she came to the corner and then took off running.

Nathan had showered, shaved and dressed meticulously for this big occasion. His new suit fit him as if the manufacturer had been his personal tailor. He had on his best white shirt and a tie that cost him more than a good reference book for his library. It was worth it.

He sat at his desk now looking over the typed manuscript of his address. It represented hours of work at his desk after other hours of research on the Revolutionary War and its hero buried outside Oclonee, the only one in this area. He intended to push every national and local patriotic stop available and give the DAR and its guests a full scale musical drama they'd not soon forget.

He laid aside the manuscript and glanced through the small neat cards containing his notes, then put them in his shirt pocket. He was about to leave, thinking to be a little early on the scene, when Josephina came running into his study without knocking.

She was not deterred by his frown but came up to his desk panting, frantic with some news.

"Josephina, you must not come into my study without knocking. You know you know better."

"I'm sorry," she panted.

"And I'm extremely busy. I'm on my way to a very important meeting." It was more than important, it was crucial. He absolutely had to have a turning point, and never in his worse nightmares had he dreamed he'd be counting on a thing like a DAR meeting for a turning point.

She swallowed. "Haven't you got just a minute? Haven't you got just one or two minutes?"

122

He looked at his watch. "One or two, that's all. What are you into now?"

"Nothing, preacher, but could you come with me and help me for just a minute?"

"Help you what, rob a bank?"

She shook her head quickly and Nathan saw a desperate look come over her face. "Uncle S. P. is sick," she said. "He's out at the school house sick, and he's spilled some paint, and he's sick.

Nathan stood up. "Josephina, if S. P. is sick you should go to Dr. Davison's office."

She grabbed both of the bottom flaps of his new coat, wrinkling them in her hands. "He's not that kind of sick."

"Oh," he said, reaching to rescue his coat. "Well, Josephina, your uncle has these . . . spells . . . every now and then. He'll feel better in a little while and go on home."

"No," she said, pulling at his coat, "he's spilled this paint and it's getting all over the auditorium floor."

He pulled her hands away from his coat and smoothed it down. "Josephina, I have to make a very important speech in just a few minutes. I can't go out to the school now. Why don't you go tell your daddy?"

"No!" She grabbed for his coat again but he caught her hands and held them. "Not my daddy. Preacher, my daddy is going to put Uncle S. P. in jail if he catches him drunk again, and there's rats there and worms in the grits . . . Wilbur says!"

Nathan didn't know what to do with the frantic little girl. He thought that S. P. probably ought to go to jail, rats or no rats, but he couldn't tell Josephina that.

"If you'd just come with me," she said, "we could get him in your car and take him home, then I could get Wilbur and we'd go clean up the paint."

"Josephina, I don't have time."

"It wouldn't take but a few minutes," she said.

He looked at his watch again. "All right," he said, resigning himself to the necessity.

When they got to the school they found the door to the auditorium open and the spilled paint but no S. P.

Nathan sighed in exasperation. "See? He's gone home." *123*

Josephina whirled around on one foot. "Let me look around," she said and ran out the door.

He waited for her, chafing, looking at his watch. She came running back in just a minute, brushing off her hands and knees.

"He's up under the stage," she said. "He's crawled through the little outside door and he's lying on the ground up under the stage. He's asleep. I tried to push him out, but he's too big."

"Well, just let him sleep," Nathan said. "When he wakes up he'll go home."

She clasped her hands together in front of her. Fixing her eyes on his she spaced her words slowly. "If you crawled very carefully, you wouldn't hardly get dirty at all."

"Josephina!"

"Oh, preacher... I can't do it by myself. He's too big. I'll put my whole savings in the collection Sunday if you'll just help."

"Josephina, it's not a matter of your having to bribe me. I'd like to help you, but be reasonable."

"Please!" she said once more, stretching her hands toward his coat.

He saw then that he could not reason with her. He took her hands and tried to start her toward the car. She balked.

"Josephina, I am not going under that stage. I can't."

"Not even to help Uncle S. P.?"

"I can't," he said, feeling desperate now himself. He showed her his watch. It was almost time for the meeting to start and he had a five minute drive to get there.

She looked at his watch sounding out the time wordlessly with her lips. Then she stood back from him looking into his face. He knew she believed at last he was not going to help her.

Her mouth trembled and she blinked her eyes. *She is going to cry,* he thought, but she didn't. She heaved her shoulders and then straightened them, accepting a burden too big for their width. She looked at the crawl space door and back at him.

"No need for me to pray," she said. "If you won't help me, God won't."

He shoved her roughly away from the door, got down on his hands and knees and began to crawl under the stage.

When Nathan finally got to the park and to the platform built for the program the Methodist minister was making some obviously impromptu remarks.

Miss Alma as president, Rena who was to have introduced him, Alberta Peeples who had no doubt sung her solo, and several strangers who were probably the officials from the state Historical Society were on the platform.

Miss Alma looked bothered and hurt and Rena looked away. Alberta smiled maliciously and the strange gentlemen stared at Nathan's suit which besides being dusty had a bright smear of green paint across the coat pocket.

Since Rena appeared to be rooted in her place the Methodist minister gave him a hasty, but under the circumstances a gracious introduction.

"I most profoundly apologize," Nathan said to the assembled DAR's and guests perspiring under the hot sun. "I was delayed by unusual circumstances which I am not at liberty to disclose."

He brushed back his hair which he had tried to comb using the car's mirror, and ran a finger under his wilted collar.

A few among the crowd seemed amused or sympathetic, but most not. Eleanor looked concerned and a little suspicious. She probably thought he had pulled this trick on purpose. He spread his notes on the lectern and began his beautifully written speech. It was no good. His being outrageously late and then arriving looking like he'd been run over by a painter's truck ruined it.

As he plodded along he would have sworn that Rena had turned her head to watch him suffer, skewering him with her black eyes to the lectern.

When the program was over he turned to speak to Miss Alma. She smiled faintly, but Rena jerked her head and started off the platform. He caught her arm.

"I'd like to try to explain."

She turned back to face him. "There's nothing you could possibly say, that would matter. You have humiliated us before the community and the Historical Society of Florida."

Miss Alma looked suddenly tearful and followed Rena off the platform.

He raised his arms and then let them fall helplessly to his sides. He gathered his notes from the lectern.

"So be it," he said.

19

"I HAVE TO GET AWAY from there," Nathan said. "I simply have to. It was a mistake for me to take that church and it's better to face it and get out."

Nathan was sitting in Paul Conyer's study in Anderson. This study had always been a frustration to him, because it was paneled and carpeted and had matched office furniture. The soft wood tones of the desk served tonight only as a muted backdrop to his own active emotion.

Paul sat back in his chair, his deep set gray eyes half curtained by the smoke circling up from his pipe. "Of course, Oclonee First has a rather evil reputation," Paul said through the smoke, "but you really haven't been there long enough to talk about moving."

Nathan jerked in his chair. "Look! Don't think I haven't told myself that a couple of million times! It's no good, I tell you. Everything I've tried to do, everything, has turned out wrong. These people have their backs up against me and they will not let me do anything right. I've spared you lots of the gruesome details, be grateful for that. I tell you the situation is impossible. I want out."

Elbows on the arms of his chair Paul linked his fingers across his chest. "Well, I still think you're giving up too soon, but as a matter of fact it had crossed my mind to recommend you to a church in Atlanta."

"Atlanta?"

Paul did not answer immediately but sat easily, looking at him with a half smile. Nathan knew Paul was playing the scene for all it was worth and him in it. "Okay, okay," he said, "what's open in Atlanta?"

"Ever heard of Whitehall?"

Nathan sat back in his chair. "Whitehall! You're kidding."

Ambitious as he was he had not considered himself in line for that prize. Large, wealthy, and with a youth and music program that had made news copy even in northern periodicals.

"I'm not kidding. A friend of mine is on their pulpit committee. He's coming down for a few days on the beach and I had thought before you came tonight of putting your name in the pot. I know what they want, and young as you are, I think you've got it."

Nathan didn't know what to say. He swallowed. He had come to Paul desperate for any kind of a church to escape to — a quarter time affair in the Okefenokee would have served — and now he saw Whitehall rising like an earthly heaven before him.

Paul laughed. "Well, for a man as full of words as you've been tonight you are very quiet."

"I may be quiet but my motor's running about 140 miles an hour."

"Well, put it in neutral, son, and let's do a little planning."

Nathan pulled his chair closer to Paul's desk. He'd be glad to do a little planning. He'd plan all night if it meant getting a church like Whitehall.

Eleanor ate sparingly of her dinner, worrying over Nathan. He had sat through the meal, morosely pushing his food around on his plate and answering her comments and Cora's with little more than monosyllables.

She knew he was bitterly disappointed with the shape of events in Oclonee. For weeks he had seemed distracted and ill tempered, but the last few days she had sensed a passing of this stage. He had begun dashing in and out of the house with his old zip and this morning she had heard him bellowing a slightly off-key fraternity song in his room.

She had known he was going to Anderson to have lunch with Paul Conyers, and was glad, since it seemed to give him such a boost. But tonight his depression had obviously returned. Eleanor watched him maneuvering green peas into a semi-circle on his plate. When he paused and looked at her absently she asked, "Is anything wrong, Nathan?"

"What? Oh, no."

"Well, you're awfully quiet tonight."

"What? Oh, nothing's wrong. Just thinking," he said, starting in on a new semi-circle with mashed potatoes.

"Well, I declare, Nathan," Cora fussed, "what ails you? I never saw you make a play pretty out of your food."

Nathan shoved his plate aside and pushed up from the table. "Good grief! You sound like my mother and sisters! I'm going over to the church where I can find some peace!"

He stomped out leaving the two women staring after him.

"Well, I never," Cora said.

"And they say women are temperamental," Eleanor sighed, more dismayed than ever. "Oh, I do hope there's nothing new wrong at the church."

Cora shook her head. "There's nothing new wrong at the church. It's that girl of his. He never gets letters from her her anymore, and I don't think he gets them at the Post Office. She just looks like the kind that would give a man fits."

Nathan did not find peace at the church though it was empty and quiet. When he could no longer bear the stillness he locked up and headed home.

Eleanor was sitting in the porch swing in a pool of light from the street lamp. One foot tucked up under her she seemed very young, and unbearably distant.

She did not stop swinging when he came up on the porch.

"Corrie already in bed?" he asked, thumping the back of a rocker to send it ruprupping back and forth.

"Mmmhummm," Eleanor said, looking beyond him down the street.

"I wanted to apologize to her and to you for tonight."

"Oh, we didn't pay any attention to that," she said, dipping down to pop a mosquito on her bare leg.

He moved quickly and catching the swing's arm stopped it. "Then why don't you look at me so I'll know you're not mad?"

Eleanor untucked the foot that was under her, crossed both feet together like a little girl at a party and offered him a saccharin smile, teasing.

129

Nathan couldn't smile back. He closed his eyes and rubbed two fingers across his eyebrows. "I am sorry," he said.

Eleanor said hesitatingly, "There is something new wrong, isn't there?"

Nathan sat on the edge of the rocker, elbows on his knees, jaws in his hands. "I'll tell you something, El'na, just you. Don't tell Corrie."

"Okay, Nathan."

"I went over to Anderson today to have lunch with Paul Conyers. He had another friend coming, a man named David Smoot from Whitehall — that's a church in Atlanta. Paul and I worked it all out ahead. I was to act as if I had just happened to come to his office by accident and didn't know Smoot would be there."

"Sounds complicated."

"Well, it is and it isn't. You see, Smoot is a deacon and a member of the pulpit committee of Whitehall and they're looking for a preacher."

Eleanor stopped the swing with both feet. "Nathan, you wouldn't leave Oclonee?"

"You don't think so? Eleanor, besides the hassle I'm in here — this church — Whitehall — it's only one of the best churches in Georgia. It's a real plum, my friend. Compared to what I've got here — well, I'll stop before I get rude."

"But you couldn't leave Oclonee, you've just come."

"Don't fret yourself. I won't leave, at least not to go to Whitehall."

"Well, why not? What happened? Don't just sit there and look glum."

"I'm not their man, that's all. I'm just not their man."

"Nathan, could you please start from the first and tell me what happened?"

Nathan sighed, beginning to wonder if he could tell, even Eleanor. "Paul knew Smoot was coming, see, and he called me to come over, but act like I came to borrow some Brotherhood material or something. He wanted me to meet Smoot under natural conditions. Hah! Smoot was supposed to be looking me over while I was supposed not to know I was being looked over.

"Paul filled me in on the facts about the church and what they wanted — young man, personable, good with young adults and with a good background. This is a rich church, see, and all these cultured church members want somebody who can mingle with them and not eat with the wrong fork."

Eleanor gave the swing a quick little push and ran her hands across the smooth hair over her ears, tucking a non-existent stray strand into the thick braid she had fashioned at the nape of her neck.

"I'm shocking you," Nathan said.

"No, no," she protested, "I'm not shocked exactly, but I've never heard a preacher talk just this way."

"Well, forget it. I don't want to talk about it anyway. I don't know why I started."

"I'm glad to listen."

"I said I don't want to talk about it."

"Well, all right, Nathan." Eleanor got up out of the swing. "I'm sorry for whatever happened to make you so miserable ... I think I'll go on to bed. Good night then, Nathan."

"Good night," he said, rocking his chair sharply back and forth.

When she had gone in he slowed the rocker and in a moment got up and moved to the end of the porch where it was dark. Leaning his forehead against a post he let the wretched memory take hold.

The meeting had gone well, the conversation guided expertly, allowing him to get in the right expressions of his conservative yet forward looking theology, his good humor, and his obviously cultured background. And in spite of the necessity of keeping his part of the conversation guarded, he had really enjoyed talking convention scuttlebutt with the fellows.

They had finished lunch and were drinking a last cup of coffee when Paul, giving him a careful wink excused himself to go to the men's room.

Nathan felt perfectly at ease — urbane — accepted by his peers. He was relaxing comfortably in his chair, savoring his sensation of well being along with his coffee when David leaned forward suddenly.

"Say, I've been trying to think all along where I've seen *131* you or who you remind me of. Now I wonder if I've got it. Some years ago when I lived in south Georgia, I crossed paths a couple of times with an old fashioned country preacher. You know — the uneducated, earthy type — but a real trash mover in the pulpit.

"It seems to me his name was something like yours, not Nathan, but a Bible name for sure, and Waite — seems like it was Waite. You remind me of him in some way. You wouldn't be related?"

Nathan fingered his napkin nervously and looked at the door of the men's room hoping Paul would appear to create a diversion.

"Hmmm," he stalled, frowning as if trying to think. Paul would not, would not come. Smoothing his napkin out he concentrated on smoothing his voice also. "I don't believe I know him," he said. "Would you like more coffee?"

A light rain was bouncing off the scraggly hedge at the edge of the yard and the grass by the porch. Baby frogs called with their tiny voices and the scent of fresh turned earth rose in the air.

"How could I have done it? How could I?" Nathan whispered against the wet wood of the post.

He leaned out over the railing, letting the pin points of rain fall on his face. With a convulsive sob he breathed in the smell of the earth.

"Complete with potter's field," he said, and wept.

20

THE NEXT DAY NATHAN stayed in his room as much as possible, pretending to work. He couldn't work, but he couldn't go out either. He felt like a peeled sapling, and wondered if he could ever grow new bark.

Cora came to his room late in the day, hesitant after several earlier rebuffs. "Brother Waite, I don't mean to bother you, but Annie Reeves is downstairs. You know I told you earlier her grandbaby died, Johnny Wilkinson's baby boy."

"Oh," he said, biting his bottom lip. Floundering in his own private swamp he had forgotten about the baby. "Just a minute, let me put a tie on."

When she had gone he hastily tied a tie and gave his hair a quick smooth with his hands. Coming down the steps he saw Annie perched on the edge of a chair like a small anxious bird. As he took her hand he said, "I heard this morning about the baby . . . I was coming later. I am sorry, I am really sorry."

Annie patted his hand. "It was for the best. The little thing would never have been well. The doctor told us that, soon's it was born. It was its heart, y'know."

Nathan drew his chair nearer hers. "How are Johnny and Annelle taking it?"

Annie's eyes brimmed with tears. "Well, Johnny ain't taking it a'tall." She sat quiet still a moment and then wiped her eyes dry. "You don't know Johnny and Annelle very well, them not being in our church. Annelle used to come regular with me 'til she married Johnny, but as you know he's not a church-going man, didn't come from a church-going family, and she drifted away. Nobody's been able to get her back."

Nathan stirred uneasily. He for one hadn't really tried.

"Lately Annelle has gone some to that tent church down by the railroad. Johnny even went once and that preacher has been to their place a couple of times.

"He seemed to be a right good preacher. He could quote scripture like it was printed on the air in front of him and Annelle said he preached powerful messages and never used no notes."

Annie glanced apologetically at Nathan.

"That's all right, Annie," he said, "not all preachers are gifted that way."

"But Brother Waite, I have to tell you, that preacher done Johnny and Annelle wrong, before God he did. Them two has been married fifteen years, and they never had no children but just Adelaide. All these years Johnny's been talking boy, boy, boy. He is right foolish about Adelaide, but he's been crazy to have a boy. Now Annelle finally had this boy and Johnny was the happiest man you ever saw. When Dr. Davison told him the boy had a bad heart Johnny just wouldn't believe it. Me and Annelle believed it. The baby from the very start had a funny color and it seemed like it never breathed easy.

"Annelle took a notion she wanted this preacher from the tent to come and pray over the baby. She said he claimed to be a healer and she wanted him to come. Johnny wouldn't hear of it because he just couldn't admit there was anything wrong with that little boy. He'd just pick him up and carry him around and say, 'Look a'here at Daddy's big man. Anybody says this boy's sick's a blame liar.'

"Well, yesterday, Johnny was at work and I was over to Annelle's washing up some diapers for her when she called, 'Mama, come quick,' and I run and when I got there she was holding the baby and a'crying and the baby was gasping. And then before I could think where to turn the little thing quit gasping and I knew it was gone."

"I didn't know, Annie. I didn't know about all of this."

"I know you didn't. I know you can't be everywhere and tend to everybody's needs. But you haven't heard the worst. Johnny got home and he near went crazy. Annelle asked me to call that tent preacher. I did it because she asked me. When he came, do you know what he said? Do you know 134 what he said to my poor Annelle and Johnny standing over their little dead baby?"

Nathan shook his head dumbly.

"He pointed to the baby and then to Johnny and Annelle and said, 'Judgment has come to your house. You've been tempting the Lord, drinking, and not going to church. Now he's taken your baby to bring you to your knees.'"

Nathan shook his head in disbelief.

"He did. And Johnny threw him out of the house. I mean he caught him by the clothes and threw him out the door and he yelled, 'Don't ever come near me or mine or I'll kill you! I'll kill any preacher comes near me or mine!'

"Now he's just sitting in the parlor where the baby's laid out and he won't let nobody, me nor Annelle nor nobody say a word to him."

"Oh, Annie, what a terrible thing to have happened to you all."

Her brown eyes brimming and spilling over Annie looked at him. "Preacher, will you come?"

Nathan shuddered. He looked down at his hands and then his feet. When he was sure he could control his voice he said, "Annie, I'll come. I may just make him worse, but I'll come."

Cora and Eleanor had been standing in the dark dining room. They came now and put their arms around Annie. Cora said, "I'll come over now too. I've got a cake I was going to bring over later anyway."

Nathan stood looking at them. "Just a minute, I'll get my coat." He ran upstairs and to his closet. Reaching in he felt the good, hard weave of his new suit, and then released it.

He shuddered again.

"I'm unable, Father. I'm unable. Help me, please."

When they came into the tiny frame house of the Wilkinson's the door to the living room was shut. Annelle was in the kitchen with some of the neighbors and friends. When he had spoken to her Nathan went back to the living room and quietly opened the door.

Johnny was sitting near the couch where the undertaker had laid the baby, his elbows on his khaki clad knees, his head in his rough fisherman's hands.

Hearing the door he looked up and stared so fiercely at Nathan that the gold flecks in his brown eyes flashed like living sparks.

"Preacher, you ain't wanted. No preacher, no sermons wanted."

"I've got no sermon, Johnny."

"Well, just turn around and go back where you come from. You never saw my baby alive. No need to see him dead."

Nathan stood still a moment and then moved a step or two into the room and stood looking at the tiny body on the couch, a perfect little face like a beautifully created doll, a soft little body, the tiny hands loosely curled, the feet in blue booties. A son lost, before he was really a son.

Johnny had risen, his whole body stiff with anger. Watching him advance Nathan's eyes blurred and he wiped at them with the backs of his hands.

Johnny stopped and grated between clenched teeth, "What you crying for, preacher? What's a fancy pants preacher like you crying for?"

"Because your baby is so beautiful. And because you wanted a son so badly and because he was yours to hold for such a little while. He's so tiny. He never learned to say your name and he'll not fish off your boat as you dreamed."

Johnny's face was gray as old ashes. He looked at the body on the couch and back to Nathan. His body had gone limp and he spoke with the voice of a dazed child. "That preacher said God killed him."

"Johnny, I'm a young man. I don't know much about anything yet. But one of the things I know, and I'd stake my eternal soul on it, God did not take your baby to punish you — what a cruel thing that would be. God is not cruel. He meant your boy to be perfect. Something went wrong somewhere. He knows your grief, because He knows about lost sons. He's lost so many, one way or another."

Nathan wiped at his face with the back of his hand. He moved slowly to Johnny and put his hands on his shoulders, looking into his face. Johnny didn't move.

"Now I want you to go and comfort your wife. She is so hurt and she needs you."

Johnny went slowly out into the hall and Nathan followed him. He knew it was all right to leave when he saw Johnny walk into the kitchen and take his wife in his arms.

21

THIS IS MY FATHER'S WORLD,
And to my listening ears,
All nat-ure sings, and round me rings
The music of the spheres.

The Junior department of the Bible school sang the words and Nathan sat in his study listening to them. He found the optimism of the child's song of worship consoling and even cheering.

Recruiting workers for the school had not been easy. Alice Stevens, who had committed herself months ago to serve as superintendent, had suddenly backed out. It seemed Buck had decided this was the time for their vacation. Alberta Peeples who had directed the music for ten years sent word she had other plans this year. He'd had the same sort of trouble getting people to visit on behalf of the revival which was the next big event on the church's schedule.

Nathan sighed, and looking at his watch decided to make a couple of quick calls himself. Coming out of the church he waved at Eleanor sitting at the edge of the church lawn with a little group of children.

And there was the brightest spot of the whole picture. Bright and beautiful. One real good reason for sticking it out in Oclonee. Eleanor and the children waved back and Nathan reluctantly moved on.

She was so perfect for him. As right as Julia had been wrong. And since she was so right it was inevitable that she would sooner or later return his love. He would wait as long as he had to.

In his car Nathan turned his mind with difficulty to the calls he should make and decided to go by the Roger's home first. Jim Rogers was a vice-president at the mill and already active in the Rotary club. Thinking of what a great addition to the church the family would make he drove by the old

Cooper house sitting silent and haunted on a bright summer's day.

Not knowing exactly why he was doing it he stopped his car and backed up along the curb to park in front of the house. The Coopers were hardly prospects — a woman who had completely withdrawn from society, and a retarded boy. He got out of the car anyway, and walked quickly up the sidewalk and onto the wooden porch. The painted floor was ringed with old blisters, the rocking chairs that no one rocked in guarded the dark varnished door.

Mrs. Cooper was a long time answering the bell, and when she did she opened the door only a little. Nathan was sure she was not going to let him in. "I'm Nathan Waite," he said. "I'm the preacher at the Baptist church."

She looked up at him with immobile face, her hand, almost transparent in its thinness, holding the door just barely open.

"I would like to come in for a moment and visit with you, or we can sit out here on the porch if you'd rather."

To his surprise she opened the door wide enough for him to pass, and when he was in motioned him to the dark living room.

He waited for her to sit down, but she stood looking at him and then pointed with one long finger to a chair. He sat down, feeling more uneasy with the passing moments. His back was to an open archway leading into another room and he felt vulnerable to whatever danger might lurk within those shadows.

"It's a pretty day," he said.

She nodded.

He looked around. It had been a fine home once. There were pieces of bisque on the mantel he knew were valuable. Remembering Josephina's tales of how Mrs. Cooper threw things from the windows he decided she was a selective thrower.

The house was absolutely quiet. The boy, or man, whoever and whatever he was, was making no sound.

"Have you been well?" he asked.

She nodded.

"The winter was mild, but I'm always glad to see summer come."

She nodded again.

This is weird, he thought. *This is absolutely weird. What do I say now?* She seemed not to care whether he talked or not, but sat watching him, a frail shadow of a woman poised on an antique chair like one of her own bisque figurines.

Knowing it sounded foolish Nathan said, "We'd like for you to come to church sometime and worship with us."

This time she did not nod, but she didn't seem to be angry either. Feeling empty of amenities he got up and offered his hand. She looked at it and then away. He dropped his hand.

"Well, I must be going. I'll come back and see you again."

This time her head moved again, but in a negative direction. "No," it said, "No."

He smiled anyway and moved to leave. She followed him, and then stood back as he opened the door to let himself out. "Good day," he said, turning, but she had shut the door behind him.

The heat struck him like a metallic shield and the smells of summer — roses and hot tar and baking salt marsh — pushed the stale scent of the house closed behind him deep in his nostrils. He had a moment of wondering which world was real.

He got in his steaming car and drove back to the church, no longer in the mood to make calls.

He sat at his desk without working, the shade of the frail recluse haunting him. How sad, he thought, how sad and how hopeless.

He swiveled his chair to face the window, trying to break the mood. Well, at least she let me in, he comforted himself, and at least she didn't throw a "coke" bottle at me.

There had been something else that was hopeful, too, some small something nagging at his conscious mind, struggling up from a deeper level, something he had seen in Mrs. Cooper's living room. In another moment the memory broke free.

In a porcelain vase on a table in the corner, "ol' lady Cooper" still kept the dried remains of Josephina's spray of Christmas greens.

The morning session of Bible School concluded, the children spewed out of the church like water from a fire hydrant.

The teachers, looking as if they had been damp dried in a machine crept out, and after a little while the building was quiet.

Nathan knew it was time for him to go home for lunch, but he had just gotten into a new text on current theological trends and gave himself another quarter hour to read. Cora would hold his lunch for him.

He was beginning to get lost on page seventeen when Eleanor's voice calling to someone outside the church found him. He closed the book. Maybe lunch couldn't wait.

Nathan grinned at his own excitement and joy just at hearing her voice, and while he was collecting a few things to take home she appeared at his door.

Bowing low he directed her to a chair with an exaggerated sweep of his arm. "And to what may I attribute the honor of this call, Sister Boyette? Bible School driven you mad? Your great Aunt Bessie's third cousin twice removed want me to call on her mother-in-law's brother-in-law?"

"Oh, Nathan." She laughed and came toward him, her eyes bright with some excitement. Pausing before his desk she fidgeted a moment and then thrust a letter in his hand.

Nathan raised his eyebrows seeing an Anderson postmark. "Read it," she said.

He unfolded the plain bond paper and read a note written in angular script.

> Dearest Eleanor,
> I'm wondering if you would care to attend the next concert in Anderson with me? The Baltimore Symphony is appearing the second Saturday in August.
> I realize you cannot do such a thing without careful thought. (Cora will jump to certain conclusions and Oclonee will assuredly follow.) I am, however, asking you to do that careful thinking.
> It would be so wonderful to spend an evening with you again, Eleanor — almost like old times.
> Hoping to have an affirmative answer from you soon,
> > I remain your devoted,
> > Buddy

Nathan read the note through twice and couldn't look up. He put his head in his hands, still staring at the words.

"Nathan?"

"Hmmm?"

"What do you think it means?"

There was no mistaking the hope in her voice. Nathan pushed the letter away with a quick sweep of his hand. Eleanor jumped at the suddenness of his move.

He spoke to her with a coldness he knew was cruel. "It means exactly what you hope it means. He's starting up the music and when he thinks the proper time has elapsed he is going to ask you to get on the merry-go-round again. Only this time, I hope he stays on it with you."

Eleanor stared at him, shocked disbelief in her eyes, but he could not stop.

"And don't look at me like I'm your mean old step-father. You've mooned over this guy forever and now at last you're going to become his lawfully wedded wife."

She put her hands to her face — not crying — just sitting there looking at him, holding her hands to her face, as if to keep it from falling away.

After a dreadful moment she stood up and said in a small voice, "I'm sorry I troubled you, today and the other times. I thought we were friends." She looked toward the portrait of Julia Harrison that he'd long since moved from his bedroom to his study desk. "I thought you would understand because you were in love yourself."

In cold fury Nathan caught up the picture and holding it high, dropped it crashing into his waste basket.

Eleanor's chin dropped. "Your fiancee . . ." she murmured.

Nathan felt as if he'd like to pick her up and send her after the picture. "My dear Miss Eleanor Boyette, I have no fiancee."

She looked at the wreckage in the waste can.

"That stupid picture belongs to my seminary roommate — his sister, no less."

"But you told Corrie . . ."

"I didn't tell Corrie anything. She saw that picture and asked me if it was my intended. I just said something like 'intended is a good word.' She took it from there. I admit I meant her to. It promised to give me some needed protection from the local belles — and later — it seemed to make it possible for you and me to have a relaxed relationship."

"And you haven't been in love at all?"

Nathan turned his chair to face out the window, the anger he had felt no longer sustaining him. In a moment he swiveled back to face her. "El'na, I have been in love, for a good little while."

"But who?"

"You'll have to admit the supply is limited."

The color which had drained from her face earlier now rushed back.

"Nathan, no."

"Yes, yes, oh my, yes."

Eleanor put her hands to her face again. "I'm an idiot. I don't know what to say."

Nathan folded the letter and placed it in its envelope. "El'na, I want you to be happy. Buddy seems to be your happiness and I must accept that and I do."

She clasped her hands together, stretching them to him. "Nathan, you're the dearest, sweetest friend I've ever had in the world. I'll always love you as my dearest friend."

He smiled. "I'll accept that for the comfort you meant it to be." He got up abruptly. "Look, I've got a little more reading I want to do before lunch. Why don't you scoot home and tell Corrie I'll be there shortly?"

She came to him and put her hand on his arm. "Nathan?"

He could not bear her nearness. "Scoot, girl, scoot."

Nathan put his elbows on his desk, folded his hands over the back of his head and sat hunched around the pain in his chest.

Why should I feel this way? What did I expect? Really. On what basis did I hope? I've been her Father Confessor. Of all people I should have known how she felt about Buddy.

The note appeared before his eyes like a framed picture. The second Saturday in August. Right at the end of the revival. Maybe she wouldn't go. Maybe knowing how important the revival was to him she wouldn't go.

He pulled his head down closer to his chest. *She will go. She will go.*

Jerking up suddenly he swiveled around to see if he could 142 get a glimpse of her moving toward the house next door, but she was not there.

She will go, he said again.

22

ON A WEDNESDAY NIGHT in August Nathan sat on the platform by Jesse Steele, uncomfortable physically and mentally — mentally because the crowd was poor and physically because he was hot. The air-conditioning system, already inadequate because the church had tried to "save money," had conked out completely sometime after last night's service.

The night was unusually still with only an occasional breeze rattling the palm branches outside the church on its way in. Dozens of hastily collected palmetto and funeral parlor fans waved in the hands of men and women alike. Children read the funeral parlor's commercial on the backs of the fans, chewed the corners into pulp or sat picking at the staples holding the cardboard backs to the wooden handles.

The meeting, begun on Sunday, had not yet drawn a really good crowd in spite of the fame and flair of the visiting evangelist or the fact that the song leader played the guitar.

Nathan had appealed to those present last night that they contact absentees in behalf of the revival. After the service Rena had provided her special brand of encouragement.

Standing like a Maypole in a circling group of women she had called out, "Reverend Waite, when Brother LeRoy was our minister the crowds filled the balcony."

When the group had turned away he had mimicked her under his breath, *"Reverend* Waite, *Brother* LeRoy . . ."

Tonight's crowd was the smallest yet. Of greater concern to Nathan was the fact that thus far no decisions had been made, at least no public ones; no conversions, no applications for church membership, no rededication of life.

Maybe the critics had it right. Maybe the day of the revival was past. Maybe it was a hopelessly old fashioned idea, that a special time should be set aside to emphasize the individual's need to make a personal commitment to Christ and his way of life, and to witness to that commitment publicly.

He looked around the congregation. There were a few present who needed to make this commitment for the first time — several children, and Annelle Wilkinson was there, sitting with her mother, but not Johnny. Johnny was out in front of the church in his car. He could watch and hear most of the service if he wanted to, which Nathan doubted.

But actually, the large majority of those present were long time Christians sitting dispassionately on pews accustomed to their peculiar weight. Looking into their faces Nathan could put names to some of the pounds — selfishness, pride, greed, vindictiveness, suspicion, indifference, boredom . . .

For these church members and for the others who were home watching the small picture, revival had to be pertinent — old fashioned, yes, irrelevant, no. What the church needed to do was rip out the pews. If any pew at all was needed it ought to be a giant sized mourner's bench.

When the service was over he found Rena waiting for him in his study. It was the first private encounter they'd had since the DAR fiasco.

He did not ask her to sit down.

"This is the least effective revival we've ever had," she said, not bothering with preliminaries.

"We've got one of the best evangelists in the country," he defended.

"The best man in the country can do nothing against hard-hearted and stiff-necked Christians."

That wasn't a new idea to him. "Are you speaking generally or specifically?"

"Reverend Waite! Why won't you see what is so obviously at the root of all our trouble? How can you stand in our pulpit Sunday after Sunday and look complacently at the Lesters and Thompsons, so tragically estranged after years of friendship? How can you treat Bill Thompson as if he were perfectly acceptable to you? Why do you look with unconcern into the face of the young woman who seduced that young man, split the home and ruptured those parent's friendship?"

"Assuming those are not just rhetorical questions I will try to answer them. I do not look at the divided families complacently, I am concerned for them. When I look at Bill I see a young man who is as repentant as any sinner I ever met, and I devoutly hope that he and Effie may yet be reconciled. But when I look for the guilty young woman I am at a loss. I simply don't know who she is."

"Do you seriously expect me to believe that Cora Haynie has never told you who she is?"

"I can't help what you do or don't believe, seriously or otherwise, Mrs. Petrie. I don't know who the girl is. I've never considered it my business to know, really. I can't fathom why you persist in making it yours."

Rena stretched herself upward, towering in her anger. "As a Christian and a mother, it is certainly my business. God forgive you that you don't think it's your's also."

She drew a deep breath, expanding her bosom, and prepared to leave.

"I have completely given up on you, Reverend Waite, I will say it to your face, and as of this night there is something else that I am going to make my business. I am sorry that you have forced me to this position. Good night, Reverend Waite."

On Friday afternoon Nathan walked back into the kitchen where Cora was preparing supper with a minimal amount of pot banging.

He knew something was wrong by the way she moved and the way she held her mouth as if she had something in there she wanted to eschew and couldn't.

He watched her a little while before he asked, "All right, Corrie, out with it, what's happened now?"

She moved a pan off the stove and turned to him, her eyes wide with distress. "Do, Lord . . . I'd rather take a beating than tell you."

"I believe you . . . what is it?"

She sucked in air through rigid jaws as if it hurt her to breathe. "There's a petition circulating. It hasn't come to me or Myrtle, but Joe heard about it at the barber shop. It's a petition asking you to resign at the end of the year, your first year."

145

She folded her hands in her apron and watched him anxiously, but he couldn't react. He felt his insides quake and burn and he did not know whether he wanted to yell or to weep. When he was sure he would do neither he asked, "Do you know who started it?"

Cora hung her head, twisting her hands in her apron.

"Never mind," he said, "I know. Rena made threatening noises the other night, and she's the only one who feels that violently about me." He stopped short, a new humiliation sweeping over him. "Except of course, if people are signing it, then we have a whole new ball game."

"I can't think many would sign it," she said — unconvincingly. "The Lesters maybe and the Becks and I heard Alberta Peeples." She paused. "And I heard, but I don't believe it, Buck. I heard Buck."

Nathan stood quietly absorbing the impact of that possibility. After a moment he said, "Now Corrie, you just put it out of your mind. I'm glad you told me. I had to know. But now it's no longer your problem."

He went over and putting one arm around her plump shoulders gave her a quick squeeze. "You're an awful nice landlady, y'know."

"Oh, preacher!" She lifted her apron to cover her face.

He left the kitchen quickly and as he started upstairs Eleanor came in. "Hi, hon," he said, hurrying to pass her.

She laid her hand on his arm and he stopped. Without looking at her he asked, "Do you know about the petition?"

When she didn't answer audibly he had to look at her. She smiled. "Don't take it too seriously," she said. "It represents only a small minority."

"Small but deadly."

"I wouldn't bet on that. I suspect this petition may put you in the underdog's role, if you'll forgive the analogy. You know how people rush to protect the underdog."

"Or to tear him to shreds."

She slapped his arm smartly. "Now you stop that. Melodrama doesn't become you."

He covered her hand with his and smiling, held it. "Yes, ma'am. Now that you've got me in line you'd better go see what you can do for Corrie."

Eleanor slipped her hand from under his and walked back to the kitchen. As soon as she got in the door Cora burst out, "Now you see what it's come to? You see what I've done? I been so busy protecting some other folks I've just about ruint my preacher!" She banged a pot on the stove. "Is that right? I'm asking you, is that right?"

Nathan waited a moment, but if Eleanor answered he didn't hear what she said.

In his room he looked at himself in the mirror, his shirt limp against his neck, his suit spiritless.

"Well, Brother Waite," he spoke softly. "It's been short and not so sweet."

He moved to his window to look out at the church, the lines of its squareness softened by a summer's moon.

It can't end this way, he protested. *It's unthinkable that it end this way. I've hardly begun.*

"Do Lord . . ." he whispered, lapsing unconsciously into Cora's cry of distress, "don't let me do this to Papa."

At supper that night Nathan determinedly demonstrated a calm acceptance of circumstances. As the meal progressed in unusual silence — the necessary remarks spoken by each of them with an elaborate courtesy — he realized that they were all three making the same concentrated effort.

It would be funny, if it weren't so painful, he thought.

Cora seemed to be having the most trouble and suddenly her control snapped. "Did she have to start it during the revival? Did she have to?"

"Of course," Nathan said. "She had to do it when it would create the most havoc."

"I think the pure devil has got into her," Cora said.

Nathan nodded. *And for once he's met his match.*

Then there was quiet again except that this time the emotions that they felt were as obvious as a fourth person at the table. And now it was Eleanor who put words to her feelings. "And there's the picnic tomorrow. Fun, food, and fellowship for all — what a farce!"

"I hadn't thought about the picnic," Nathan said, "I'd like to cancel it.

Cora stopped her fork halfway to her mouth and stared at them open-mouthed.

"Cancel the picnic? Cancel the annual church picnic?"

Nathan looked at Eleanor and they both laughed.

"Think of the kids," Cora said defensively, and Nathan leaned over to give her a reassuring pat.

The telephone rang. Neither of them moved to answer it at first, then Cora pushed up. "I'll get it."

Nathan took a swallow of iced tea to try to ease down the constriction in his throat. "Whoever it is," he said, "tell 'em to think of the kids."

It was Mr. Parker. Nathan took the telephone from Cora and they both raised their eyebrows, puzzled.

"Worth wants to see you," Mr. Parker said.

"Are you sure?"

"Yes, come over in the morning if you can."

Mr. Parker did not sound anxious or afraid, or angry, certainly not angry. Amazed? Expectant?

"I can't come in the morning, Mr. Parker, we're having our church picnic, but I could get there in the early afternoon — unless, of course, it's an emergency."

"No, it's not an emergency. Tomorrow afternoon will be fine. We'll be waiting for you."

23

SATURDAY MORNING CORA was up at dawn putting her
fryers to soak in buttermilk, peeling potatoes for salad. She
hurried Nathan and Eleanor through breakfast, giving them
orders, trying not to see the way Nathan looked at Eleanor,
the way he had been looking at Eleanor lately.

She tried to speak cheerfully and even hummed a little
hoping to start the kids off happily on what she felt personally was bound to be a very trying day. She fully expected
Rena to come with a copy of the petition rolled up in her
bosom.

By nine cars were lining up by the church loaded with
children, picnic baskets and play pens. When the rented
truck left the church loaded with supplies and teenagers her
spirits lifted — she felt somehow justified.

Saturday had dawned a hot sun, blue sky, mild breeze kind
of day. At the beach the sand gleamed clean and white.
Purple and white blossoms bloomed on vines running over
the dunes, and sea oats waved at their summits. The deep blue
ocean rolled in and boiled white along the breaker line.

Inside the pavilion long tables held grease stained paper
bags and boxes of fried chicken and casseroles of macaroni
and cheese, and rice cooked with shrimp. There was potato
salad and deep pans of green beans cooked with ham, cakes
piled high with icing, and pies — apple, chocolate and lemon
meringue pies.

After Cora had helped Myrtle make the lemonade she left
the pavilion to join the crowd on the beach.

Some of the men and the older children were swimming in
water to their shoulders. The younger ones played in the *149*
shallows, running at the waves and away from them. A gang
of little boys rolled down the dunes, shrieking, and along the

tide line Josephina and Adelaide collected shells, their skirts scooped up to hold the treasure.

Cora sighed. *Life's meant to be good and sweet,* she thought, *how come we have to mess it up all the time?*

She kicked off her shoes and walked down to the water where Alice was wading with Pauline and Dolly. For the first time Cora noticed that Buck had not come.

Dolly giggled, ankle deep in foam and sand. "We're as bad as the kids."

"But don't it feel good?" Cora said, wading in. She looked back up the beach where some of the older women were sitting on plastic strapped chairs shading their eyes under straw hats bedecked with flowers or more down-to-earth caps with bills. Miss Alma was there, under an umbrella, and by her side Eleanor shared the umbrella's shadow.

Cora folded her lips in unhappily. She knew why Eleanor didn't want to get sunburned. She had this big date with Buddy tonight and she was protecting her face.

Cora sighed again and looked to where Nathan, in white slacks, played beach tennis with some of the boys. *Do Lord,* she thought, *don't let him have more than a brotherly love for her. 'Cause sure as he's born that's all she has for him.*

While she watched him the ball game finished and he came down to the water, rolling up his pants legs as he came.

"Why don't you go swimming?" Alice asked.

"Oh, I thought I'd stay flexible," he said, "mix and mingle, keep traffic flowing smoothly."

"That sounds too busy for a picnic," Pauline said.

"You're probably right," he agreed. "What we need most is to relax."

"You're too late," Dolly said nervously. She nodded to where Rena was bearing down on them, well corseted and with shoes firmly buckled on. "I think I'll go see about Josephina."

Cora put her hand on Dolly's arm, holding her in her place.

A wave rippled in to curl around their feet and suck the sand from beneath them going out.

Rena arrived fussing. "Pauline, do you think it's wise for you to be in the water?" Without waiting for an answer she turned to Cora. "I'll declare, she looks so peaked. I thought she'd gain some weight after she got married, and especially now that she's pregnant."

Pauline started and blushed.

"Oh, now, you don't mind these folks knowing," Rena said, "especially Cora, if she doesn't know it already. She has a way of knowing things, more things than she'll ever tell."

Cora switched her skirt tighter around her knees and moved a step deeper into the water. "Let's not start that today, Rena."

"I'm not starting, Cora Haynie — I've never stopped. I'll not stop until I locate that creature and see she's punished." She turned to glare at Nathan. "In spite of all obstacles."

Dolly giggled and Cora shook her. The preacher didn't answer, just looked out across the ocean.

"Maybe she's been punished already, Mama." Pauline spoke just above the noise of the water.

"How could she be?"

"Well, I mean the shame and worry. Maybe she can't eat right or sleep sound for being sorry and afraid. Maybe if she's married she can't look at her husband without being afraid he'll find out."

"Humph," Rena snorted. "You can bet your life that type of woman is not feeling any such way."

Cora was feeling sick. Where would it end? Would it just go on and on, getting worse, entangling more people like it had entangled Nathan? Would it be better at this time of revival to get it all out and have it all done with?

She hung her head and studied her feet where the last wave had receded leaving them half buried in the sand. Moving, she stood on a cleanly washed, firm place. She stared hard at the sand. It fitted in somehow. Where?

And then Cora knew and never doubted her knowledge for a second. The Lord had reached smack out of heaven in her moment of weakness to give her a sign, just like He did for people in the Bible.

"Well, of course," she said aloud.

They looked at her, wondering.

"The answer is right there in the Bible, Rena. I'm surprised you never thought of it," she said. *151*

"Don't you dare preach to me!"

"I wouldn't try, Rena, but being here on this beach makes me think of the time those men brought that poor girl caught in adultery to Jesus." Looking at the girls she went on. "He didn't say nothing at all, but just wrote in the sand."

She pulled her heel across the wet sand at her feet making random scrolls and twirls. "Jesus asked the men who didn't consider themselves sinners to start throwing the stones, and don't you know those men all left without throwing a single stone! Jesus put His arm around the sorrowful girl and said, 'These men don't condemn you, and neither do I. God's seen your heart and forgiven you. Go in peace.'"

Rena started to speak, but a wild wave breaking large and running free came up the beach and covered their feet. Rena shrieked and ran.

The others didn't move. The water rushing back to the sea churned the sand under their heels. When it had gone the sand glistened smooth and white.

The preacher turned to her and laid his hand on her shoulder. "You preach a pretty good sermon," he said.

"I had a pretty good sign," she answered.

It was the preacher's turn to ask "What?" and hers to answer, "Nothing."

When they got home early that afternoon, stiff skinned from the salt air, broiled pink by the sun, Cora set her load of dishes on the drain board and turned to take what Nathan was carrying.

"Preacher?"

"Hmmm?"

"I got some good news for you."

"El'na's not going to Anderson," he said instantly.

"No, I'm sorry . . . but this is still good news." She smiled. "You can forget about the petition. It's been stopped."

His chin dropped a little. "No kidding? Who stopped it?"

And now she grinned. "Sam Petrie."

Mr. Parker met Nathan at the door and ushered him into the big, dim entry hall with obvious happiness. "Worth wanted you to know about a decision he has made. I think it's a good one."

They walked through the hall and when they entered Worth's room he was watching for them to come.

"Hello, preacher," he said.

"Hello, Worth." Nathan walked toward the bed a little gingerly.

"You don't have to be afraid. I'm harmless." Worth smiled and the smile was awkward on his face. He was paler than ever, but there was a difference in his looks. Some energy flowed through his still body and sparked from his eyes.

"Did you tell him?" he asked his father.

"No, it's a little new to me yet. You'd better tell him."

"I'm going back North," Worth said. "I'm going back to take up with my college work where I left off. I'll have to be privately tutored, of course, and it'll take time and money, but I've got lots of time and my father is willing to pay."

"Of course, I'll pay," Mr. Parker cried.

"I'm going to finish my education. I don't know just how I'm going to use it, but . . ." his blue-black eyes held Nathan's, "I know I will. Somehow, I know I will."

Nathan moved to the bed and grasped the thin arm tightly. "Worth, you will! There's got to be a way."

Worth laughed and a little of his old bitterness was in the laugh. "You see, father? I told you he was a man of faith. I always knew he was a man of faith somewhere behind that preacher boy stance."

Nathan's grasp loosened.

"I'm sorry," Worth said quickly. "I'm by habit such a hellion it'll take me awhile to act otherwise."

Nathan gave Worth a rough pat and then put his hands in his pockets. "Well, I'm just grateful you're talking to me."

"Yeah," Worth said, "who knows, we might even work up a friendship someday." He paused. "Annie knows I'm going back North. She says she'll pray for me." He smiled, very slightly sarcastic. "Will you pray for me, preacher?"

Nathan returned the smile. "Of course, my atheistic friend."

Worth smiled again, this time with a slow sadness. "I'm not an atheist, Nathan. Didn't you know that?"

"How long have you known it?"

"Oh . . . it kind of crept up on me. I think it started the first time I really cursed Annie. She's so religious — I thought she'd quit. Instead she brought me a cup of coffee." He closed his eyes and spoke almost in a whisper. "I determined then to run her off. I cursed her 'til her tears splashed on my face and my own ran in pure frustration. She never stopped tending me. I knew . . . after awhile . . . there couldn't be a person like Annie unless there was a God."

Mr. Parker left the room. Worth turned his face to the window. "I'm tired now," he said. "I didn't sleep last night."

Nathan put both hands on the still arm nearest him and held on hard a moment.

"I'll be going now, Worth. I'll come again before you leave." He slipped out quietly.

24

THAT NIGHT AT CHURCH when the invitation was given Nathan knew what he wanted to do. He spoke to the evangelist and at the end of the first stanza of the hymn Jesse signaled the song leader to pause in the singing.

Nathan stood in the center of the church in front of the communion table, and looked through the congregation. There were a number of empty seats, but the one next to Cora seemed as bleak as a beach deserted in winter. Eleanor had left for the concert in Anderson and by morning all Oclonee would know she was Buddy's girl again.

Cora's face was a portrait of sympathy. Nathan took a firm hold on his hymn book and spoke quietly to his people.

"The invitation time is a time we invite those who have never professed their faith in Christ to come forward acknowledging Him publicly as Lord. We also invite Christians to make it a time of confession of sins and rededication of life.

"I stand before you and the Lord tonight confessing my own sins as I should have done before now. I have been a prodigal in a far place — proud where I should have been ashamed and ashamed where I should have been proud. I have been both selfish and arrogant in my dealings with this people. I stand humbled before you tonight, and please God, I want to stay that way, to be His servant, and yours."

Cora had begun to weep and Nathan saw Buck drop his head and cover his eyes with his hand. Nathan opened his hymnal and nodded to the pianist.

> Just as I am, and waiting not
> To rid my soul of one dark blot,
> To Thee whose blood can cleanse each spot,
> O Lamb of God, I come ! I come !

The screened door of the church slammed smartly and

down the aisle came Johnny Wilkinson, in a hurry. Wide-eyed and smiling he shook Nathan's hand furiously.

"Hallelujah!" cried the evangelist. "Sing on!"

> Just as I am, though tossed about
> With many a conflict, many a doubt,

Annelle left her mother's side and started down the aisle. She was smiling nervously, but she was happy. Anyone could see that Annelle Wilkinson was happy.

The song leader called a new hymn and men and women, weeping openly, sang through their tears.

> We praise Thee, O God!
> for the Son of Thy love,

When Nathan had seated Johnny and Annelle he looked out again over the church and saw that someone else had come in. She stood in the shadow of one of the little alcoves at the back of the church.

Eleanor had come back. She had started to Anderson with Buddy, he had seen her start, but she had come back.

As he stared at her across the heads of his people, she stretched out her arms to him in the half shadow. He looked long at her, as the people sang, as if by the very looking he could answer a desperate longing in his heart.

A figure stepped from one of the rear pews and moved across the back of the church. Effie Thompson, with head ducked, walked in front of where Eleanor was standing and into a side aisle. Heads turned to follow her progress. She stopped at the pew where Bill was standing. He looked at her in wonder. She moved into the pew to his side, put her arm around him and her wet face to his cheek.

"Well, glory be!" Bill cried out loud and clutched her in a fierce embrace.

> Hal-le-lu-jah ! Thine the glo-ry,
> Hal-le-lu-jah ! amen;
> Hal-le-lu-jah ! Thine the glo-ry,
> Re-vive us a-gain.

Nathan sang at the top of his voice, his heart full like those of the other saints of First Baptist — almost all of the saints of First Baptist. Half-way back in the church he saw that Rena was not singing. Head high, chin rigid, she glared her way through the final notes of the hymn.

As the service closed the people turned in their pews to shake hands with those near them, and then moved into the aisles, jostling and crowding together, some still wiping at wet eyes, and then trying all at once to get down the aisle to speak to him.

Nathan clutched at their offered hands, murmured answers to the things they were saying, all the while straining over and between their heads to get a glimpse of Eleanor. She had made her way through the crowd to Cora's side and he saw Cora grab her in a crushing hug.

Nathan could not get away from his people; they circled him, pressed his hand, patted his back, promised their support. Eleanor stood for a while in the protection of a pew, waiting. When between heads he could see her face she motioned that she was going home and smiled that wide, lovely smile.

"Darling," he whispered fiercely, and felt the hand he was shaking jump. He looked down into the startled face of Bessie Poole. "Oh, Bessie," he murmured, as confused as she, "sorry . . ."

Buck came to him and started to speak but instead threw an arm around him and hugged him hard. When he could look up again Eleanor had gone, and Rena was coming down the aisle, dragging Pauline like a will-less rag doll. She did not stop to shake his hand. Nathan groaned audibly. Rena was headed for his study.

He put it off as long as he could, chatting with the last of his members, personally seeing the evangelist and song leader to their cars, hoping Rena would go away, but when he had no further excuse to avoid the study he went in and she was there, waiting by his desk. Pauline stood in a far corner.

Nathan faced Rena and at first they had nothing to say to each other. He waited her out and at last she spoke.

"I'm glad for the beginning we have made in this church tonight."

He nodded silently. He was so full and so empty.

"I am duty bound," she said, "under the leadership of the Spirit to bring this up one final time."

Nathan did not have to ask what it was she was going to bring up.

"We have begun, we must go all the way. The church must be cleansed."

Nathan sighed deeply. "Rena, what possible good can you accomplish by pressing this thing? Effie has forgiven Bill and to reopen the wound by bringing the other woman back into the picture can only cause fresh suffering."

Rena's face grew tight with purpose. "The Bible is clear in its teaching on adultery."

"And we were reminded on the beach today of its teaching on forgiveness."

She stared at him with a mixture of scorn and hate contorting her face.

Nathan put his hands on the back of a chair and shook it in its place to hide the trembling of his own body. Releasing the chair so suddenly that it teetered and almost fell he cried, "What is driving you, Rena? What in the name of our Lord, is driving you? Have you no heart? Can't you see that Cora and Bill have protected this girl in simple Christian compassion? Don't you appreciate the decency in that? Wouldn't you want the same decency if it had been your daughter involved? Rena — think — suppose it had been Pauline?"

He stopped, his arms outstretched, the words he had said echoing away from him like circles from a stone thrown in water, and as if caught by the farthest circle and drawn in by it, Kenny Beck appeared in the door.

He stood grinning at his mother-in-law without humor. "Yeah, Rena," he said, "suppose it was Pauline?"

Pauline sank with a little sighing sound into a chair. Nathan stepped to her side and as he put his hand on her trembling shoulder, the question he had flung in the air took the size and shape of a dreadful reality.

God in heaven, he prayed, *help Kenny to be a man.*

Kenny came to stand in front of Rena. "Suppose it was Pauline?" he asked again. Hooking his thumbs in his belt he looked her up and down, taking her measure. "And just who made you judge of the world?"

Rena gasped in utter outrage.

158

She doesn't see it yet, Nathan thought, *she still doesn't see it.*

Kenny turned to face Pauline and Nathan instinctively moved closer to her and tightened his grip on her shoulder.

Kenny saw the gesture and smiled wryly. "Thanks, preacher, but she'll be all right." He leaned over and taking both of Pauline's hands pulled her to her feet. Still holding her hands and looking into her face he said, very softly, "This here's my girl."

And then as if neither Nathan or Rena were there the young couple left the room together.

Nathan looked back at Rena. Her expression of outrage was changing slowly to one of abstruse shock. *She's getting it,* Nathan thought, *she's getting it now . . .* and even as he thought it she rared like an animal trying to throw off the dart piercing its flesh. "Indeed!" she snorted, thrashing against the pain. As he watched she began to go limp . . . not all at once, but with little jerks, until at last she stood quietly, propping herself against his desk. Her large pocketbook, so much a part of her, slipped from her fingers to fall on the floor.

And now it was Rena who was vulnerable. Now this woman who had given him a taste of hell was having to hold the cup to her own lips. And he could make her drink. And she knew it.

"What will you do?" she whispered, looking down at her feet and not at him.

She seemed to Nathan no larger than his mother. "I won't do anything," he said. "I have no stones to throw. Not at Pauline, not at you."

Accepting that as if not quite able yet to absorb it she asked dully, "What must I do?"

He walked over to where her pocketbook had fallen and picking it up closed her hand over its handle.

"I'm not sure you should do anything at all, Rena, except maybe just go home and think a long time about all that's happened, and about forgiveness. Think about forgiveness."

She moved slowly and heavily to leave his study. Hesitating at the door she looked back at him. "Good night, then, Brother Waite."

He smiled faintly. "Good night . . . my sister," he said.

Sighing, he moved to close the window behind his desk and then stopped, staring at the house next door. Suddenly, somewhere deep inside him joy broke free, and he started from the study on a run.

There was no reason to wait — he knew without looking, his desk was in order.